A FEW MINUTES PAST MIDNIGHT

A TOBY PETERS MYSTERY

Stuart M. Kaminsky

An Otto Penzler Book

CARROLL & GRAF PUBLISHERS, INC.

NEW YORK

First Carroll & Graf edition 2001

Carroll & Graf Publishers, Inc.
A Division of Avalon Publishing Group
19 West 21ˢᵗ Street
New York, NY 10010-6805

Library of Congress Cataloging-in-Publication Data
is available.
ISBN: 0-7867-0862-X

Manufactured in the United States of America

This book is dedicated to Alysha, Allison, and Bill Wargo

PROLOGUE

I SAT WITH my back against the cool headstone over the grave of one Samuel Sidney Talevest. It was dark. It was cold and somewhere in the night a man with my gun and a flashlight was looking for me.

His plan was simple: to kill me and get what I had in my pocket. My plan was simple: to stay alive. One of us was not going to be happy.

I could make out headstones and a few trees. Maybe a few feet behind the headstone my back was against, he stood waiting, listening. Something slithered through the nearby grass. I held my breath.

Then, footsteps. At least I thought I heard footsteps. They were behind me. I couldn't tell how far. Suddenly I saw the beam of his flashlight to my left. It swept from left to right and then moved forward. He was systematically going down each row, looking behind each stone.

The cemetery wasn't small, but it wasn't as big as I would have liked. And the stone wall around the place was about ten feet high. On my best day, at the age of eighteen, I couldn't have made it up and over that wall. Pushing fifty with a sore ankle, my chances hadn't improved.

I didn't see how things could get much worse.

Then it started to rain.

He didn't have all night to look. The police would be coming soon. But he was moving fast now and the odds were good that he would get to me before the cavalry arrived.

I had a little time to try to come up with something. I couldn't. I could have done a lot of things differently. I should have done a lot of things differently.

You can make up your own mind about that.

It had all started four days ago.

CHAPTER

1

"IT WAS A few minutes past midnight," Charlie Chaplin had told me sitting in an overstuffed chair in his living room.

He was wearing dark slacks, a white knit sweater, and tennis shoes. He twirled a tennis racket in his hands as he spoke. His thick, mostly white head of curly hair needed a trim. Chaplin looked at the racket and then turned his tired blue eyes to me before continuing in precise, clearly spoken words with just a hint of an English accent as he paced the living room of his house in Bel Air.

"I couldn't sleep," he continued. "I don't sleep at all well when I'm working on a new film or considering one for that matter. I happened to be sitting on the stairs near the Chinese gong on the first landing. I heard a knock. Distinct, five times, not loud. I wondered how my visitor had gotten past the gate. Given my recent problems, Mr. Peters, I've been rather more bothered by the press and the morbidly curious."

"Call me Toby," I said.

"I shall," said Chaplin not telling me what to call him. "Mr. Chaplin" would be fine for now.

He paused and looked at me, trying to decide if I was the right bill of goods. I had met him briefly once before while working on a case. I was surprised he had remembered my name and called me. Maybe I make a better impression than I think I do. Maybe. He was silent, studying me. I knew what he was looking at.

Seated in the chair across from him was a rumpled private detective with a battered face and flattened nose, a forty-eight-year-old wreck with dark hair beginning to show gray. A wreck with a bad back and some bills to pay.

I'm a good listener. I know how to keep secrets. I'm not the brightest you can buy, but I come relatively cheap and I don't give up on a client. I also know when to keep my mouth shut.

"I opened the door," Chaplin went on, apparently satisfied with what he saw. "There he stood, a slight man about forty years old, drenched, dark hair hanging over his eyes and in his right hand he held a singularly sinister and quite long-bladed knife, almost a sword really. I should have been afraid I suppose. The effect was worthy of theatrical appreciation—especially since there had been no rain. That was the perfect touch."

Chaplin was still pacing. He took a halfhearted overhand stroke with his racket. Fanny Brice or Baby Sandy could have returned it for a kill.

"I should have been afraid," said Chaplin, continuing to pace. "Perhaps at some level I was. But I was transfixed. It was as if I had been expecting him or someone like him."

"You have enemies," I prompted when Chaplin paused.

"Enemies," he said with a sigh. "You read the newspapers?" The question was accompanied by an arch of his right eyebrow.

I nodded.

"To say that I have enemies would be an understatement," he sighed. "Were my enemies to form a military unit, they would be quite a formidable military presence, at least in numbers if not in fighting ability."

He stopped, tucked his racket under his arm and began a countdown with his fingers. I fished the notebook out of my jacket, found my pencil that had already made its pointed way an inch into the lining, and began to take notes. I made a big "One" with a circle and a dash and waited.

"As you may know, I've just been married," he said. "My wife Oona, the daughter of . . ."

"Eugene O'Neill," I supplied.

Chaplin nodded. I knew his Mexican divorce from Paulette Goddard had gone through about a year ago. I knew a lot of things about Chaplin.

"Oona is eighteen," Chaplin said. "I have had, shall we say, semi-public relationships with a variety of young women."

We shall say, I thought. Some of those women were as young as sixteen.

"There are people who have been most vituperative about my marriages," he said. "And particularly hostile toward my current one. Fans of O'Neill, religious fanatics, moralists who know nothing of reality or our relationship have condemned me. I very much love my wife. I anticipate a large family and a reasonably happy future with Oona should I survive the slings and arrows of outrageous fortune and the occasional soaking wet and knife-wielding lunatic at my front door."

"You told her what happened?"

He closed his eyes again for an instant, smiled, and shook his head "no."

"Fortunately, at the moment she is attending a family funeral in Connecticut," he said.

"So," he said, "let us list some of those who might wish me harm. We begin with the fanatic fans of my father-in-law who, between us and in the confines of this room, himself has had more than an occasional attraction to quite young women. I'm sorry." He bowed his head. "That was petty of me. Would you like some tea?"

"No thanks," I said.

"And so," he continued, "one finger down for his lunatic fans."

One finger went down for the fans of Eugene O'Neill who were to be counted among those who might not be happy with Chaplin.

"Next," he said, standing before me. "Joan Barry."

I knew about Joan Barry but I kept my mouth shut. He had become involved with her a few months after his divorce from Paulette Goddard became final.

"Miss Barry was a . . . protégée of mine," he said. "A star-struck girl from Brooklyn. I was introduced to her by way of a letter of introduction from John Paul Getty who, as I understood it, knew her as a waitress. I tried to work with her, but she simply did not have the talent."

The way the newspapers told it—and they told it a lot— Barry, who was twenty-two or twenty-three, had had two abortions while she was with Chaplin. He'd dumped her a little over a year ago. She was pregnant again. This time she took Chaplin to court. Two months before this moment in Chaplin's living room, a jury had found against Chaplin despite the fact that blood tests proved he wasn't the father. The *Los Angeles Times* and newspapers around the world carried photographs of a glum Chaplin being fingerprinted.

"She came here, to this house, about ten or eleven months ago with a gun she had purchased in a pawnshop," Chaplin said. "I persuaded her to leave and filed an injunction against her and took her to court. She was given a train ticket out of town and a hundred dollars. She returned seven months ago, broke into this house and . . ."

"And?" I prompted when he paused.

"Let's move on," he said. "As a matter of deep conviction, last year I addressed a meeting in Madison Square Garden in New York calling for a second front in Europe to aid the Russians. I demanded that England and the United States attack from the west while Russia fought desperately, her back against the wall. Many people thought it was not my place to make such a plea. I then spoke at Carnegie Hall saying, more or less as I recall, 'Now is the best time for a second front while the Hun is so busy in Russia.'

"And then at an Arts in Russia Week dinner at the Hotel Pennsylvania I urged elimination of anti-Communist propaganda in the interest of winning the war. Since our allies do not object to our own ideas and form of government, I do not think it proper to object to theirs. While the attack on me came as no surprise, the level was overwhelming."

A second finger went down.

"That is for the fanatical anti-Communists who do not even recognize their own self-interest let alone the humanity of others. If Germany takes Russia, the Nazis will gain access to a new oil supply. This could result in extending the war for years. I'll try to be brief with the remaining seven," he said. "I've never become a citizen of the United States. I do not even consider myself English. I am, as I have said publicly and often, a citizen of the world. There are those who claim that while America has made me wealthy, I have no reservations about criticizing this country's policies even though I am not a citizen. Thus, I am that most dreaded of wartime creatures, a peacemonger. That is, I criticize all policies that do not lead to peace."

Even Stalin's? I wanted to ask.

His eyes were fixed on me as the third finger went down.

"Even those of Russia when appropriate," he said, reading my face. "I am not a communist with a small or large 'c.' I belong to no party. I understand I shall be called before the House Un-American Activities Committee because of my views. It was my impression that a person was free to say what he or she thought in the United States as long as he did not cry 'fire' in a crowded theater. But times change. In war, rights and principles are often forgotten or their existence suspended in the name of defense. It seems to me that we are most in need of those rights precisely when they are being most threatened. I was under the impression that it was those rights for which the United States and its allies were fighting. But I'm lecturing. Please forgive me. Shall we continue?"

I nodded.

"I was a supporter of Henry Wallace—an outspoken supporter. Enough said?"

I nodded again. A fourth finger went down. Wallace was not on the list of most beloved people in the United States.

"I have repeatedly declared that I am not a Jew," he went on. "Being Jewish is a matter of religion and conviction and, to some degree, heritage. My Jewish heritage is tenuous at best. I could simply be quiet. I choose not to be. There are people, not only Jewish people, who do not like my speaking out on such a delicate subject."

A fifth finger went down and he looked into my eyes. I looked back.

I was born Tobias Leo Pevsner. Jewish. I changed my name before I became a cop. My brother Phil, still a cop, is still a Pevsner. I didn't hide the fact that I was born Jewish. I just didn't advertise it. I didn't practice the religion and I didn't feel any connection to the tradition. I bought into the melting pot when I was a kid. It was a point of friction, one among many, between my brother and me.

"On to six," Chaplin said, looking from his now-clenched right fist to his left. "A man named Konrad Bercovici sued me recently claiming that I had stolen the idea for *The Great Dictator* from him, that he had submitted a proposal for a similar idea to me, and that I had returned it and then had made the film. I denied it on the stand, but my lawyers advised me to settle out of court. I did so with great reluctance. Expedience is sometimes essential in this one and only world."

"You think Bercovici . . ."

"No, I do not," said Chaplin. "He seemed quite content with the settlement, as well he should have been. But there may have been those who knew him or of him who . . . madness is often difficult to find by applying nonmad methods of thinking."

Finger six came down. Chaplin examined the four remaining fingers. His hands were small, delicate, and very clean.

"Since the outbreak of war," he said. "I have had hundreds of threats relayed by mail and phone, on the streets, and in the newspapers and on the radio. Mr. Westbrook Pegler seems particularly and morbidly interested in securing my deportation."

"You think Westbrook Pegler . . . ?"

"No," said Chaplin. "I think it possible that someone who reads Westbrook Pegler might not have the columnist's journalistic restraint."

Finger seven folded.

The words "journalistic restraint" were emphasized for the sake of irony.

"My career has been threatened," he said. "My convictions are unaltered. It is likely that if my career in this country is to continue I will have to fund my own projects. I have the funds though my resources have been strained. Before the war I could count on my production costs being covered by Japanese sales alone. Now, with much of the world market closed, to increase my working capital, I have considered accepting the lead in *The Flying Yorkshireman*, which Frank Capra has offered to me though I don't think I can work with any director but myself. I'm also trying to put together capitalization for a film version of *Shadow and Substance*, but I doubt if that will come about. There are people in the industry who want me to fail."

"Enough to kill you?"

"Enough to try to frighten me into oblivion or exile," Chaplin said, putting down finger eight. "The man with the blade at my door put on an arresting performance. Many of my Hollywood friends, including Harry Crocker and King Vidor, have abandoned me," he said with a deep sigh. "Regrettable. Inevitable as I can see now. But I can live with that. No, number nine comes from some statements I have made over the years concerning the use of the Negro as a source of easy humor in movies. I never laugh at such humor. They have suffered too much to ever be funny to me.

"Several times early in my career, and much to my regret, there were background players in blackface, particularly in several of the films I did at Essanay. And so there are people, bigots, who would gladly lynch me for my views on race. But then again those of the KKK ilk have a very long list."

The ninth finger came down. There was only one left, the pinky on Chaplin's left hand.

"I am working now on a film which I plan to call *Lady Killer*," he said. "It was suggested to me by Orson Welles. The Tramp will be gone. I will speak. The film will deal with the plight of a working man who turns to murder to feed his family. He marries women and murders them for their money. A Landru, or Bluebeard tale."

"A comedy," I said.

"Of course," he said closing his eyes and bowing. "Which brings us back to the curious visitation I had last night. The wet man with the knife said that I should cease working on the film. He said that if I continued to develop it, he would return and kill me. His precise and colorful words were, as I recall, 'I will skewer you.' And then he said something quite curious."

"What?"

"That I should stay away from Fiona Sullivan," said Chaplin, putting down his pinky, the game over.

"Who is Fiona Sullivan?" I asked.

He shook his head and said, "I haven't the faintest idea."

"Fiona Sullivan," I repeated.

"He pronounced the name quite distinctly," said Chaplin. "Repeated it, in fact."

"Long list of possible suspects," I said.

"Had I more fingers . . ." Chaplin said with a smile. "I did know a stunt man named Webster Skeetchman who had six fingers on one hand. And Harold Lloyd, as the result of an accident while filming, has fewer than ten. I can't remember exactly how many. But then Harold seems to have no enemies."

"And you called the police?"

"Moments after the apparition disappeared," said Chaplin, unclenching his fists and playing with his racket again. "They seemed monumentally disinterested and the shabbily dressed detective who came to the door indicated that he considered the possibility that I was lying the most likely of options open to him. His imagination seemed remarkably limited. I had the impression that he considered the possibilities that I had been drinking or was using drugs or that I was in search of sympathetic publicity. He was the same officer who had come when Miss Barry entered my house unbidden on those two separate occasions."

"Anything else?" I asked.

Chaplin considered and shook his head.

"I will think about it," he said. "Do you have enough to begin your search for this man?"

"I think so," I said, rising. "There are a few other possibilities. He could be an actor trying to impress you or just a nut who doesn't like your movies."

"Possibilities," Chaplin agreed.

"I'll keep the options open," I said standing. "One last thing."

"Remuneration," Chaplin said.

"Right."

"Your fee?"

"Twenty-five a day, expenses and, in this case, another twenty a day for someone to watch you and your wife if she gets back before I find this guy."

"Yes, I see. I would prefer if that aspect of this business be done with discretion."

"It will be," I said, as Chaplin extended his hand.

"I assume you would like an advance," he said.

"Yes," I said.

An advance would be nice. Then I could eat, get gas for my Crosley, pick up a new windbreaker, and pay my land-lady. An advance would be very nice.

"Will cash do?" Chaplin said, shifting his racket and reaching into his back pocket for his wallet.

"It will."

He counted off two hundred dollars in twenties and handed them to me. I pocketed them without a second count.

"I'll get back to you every day. My man, the one who'll be watching you, will introduce himself, stay out of your way, and keep his eyes open."

"That will be satisfactory. And now, Mr. Peters, I still have a friend or two and a brave face to show the world. And I have a tennis engagement."

I started across the room toward the front door.

"While I was counting," he said behind me softly. "I was reminded of the zeppelin sequence in *Hells Angels*. You know it?"

"Great movie," I said, turning back to him.

"Gripping sequence," Chaplin said. "First the Germans, hurrying to get away from the British planes, cut the line of the man in the observation car. Then, to lighten to load further in an attempt to outrun the British, the Germans unload most of their equipment. When that isn't enough, the enlisted men are ordered to jump out of the vessel to their death. Watching them step into the dark hole is unforgettable. And then one of the British flyers sacrifices himself by diving into the zeppelin. I identify with every one of those victims of war. I am haunted by that sequence. The brave and the innocent are the true victims of war."

"Pilots died making that movie," I said.

"I know," he said. "Making movies can be almost as dangerous as war."

He was lost in thought now. He gave me a private telephone number where I could reach him or leave a message. I wrote it in my book. I heard someone coming down the stairs when I went out the front door and crossed the driveway to my car. I had two hundred dollars to work with and too many leads. I'd need some help. I knew where to get it.

I hit the radio button. The Crosley backfired. It had been doing a lot of things it shouldn't have been doing for a few months now and it hated to come to life in the morning. It reminded me of me. I'd have to take it to No-Neck Arnie, the mechanic.

On the way back to my office going down Hollywood Boulevard, I listened to the end of *Big Sister* and caught the news. It was December 10, 1943. The announcer with the deep voice said that the war news was good. The nine-day "Battle of the Clouds" over Germany marked a major victory for United States and Canadian pilots. The Fifth Army was moving on Via Casilini. Bulgaria was getting ready to bail out on the Nazis. In the Pacific, Allied forces led by the Australians were clearing the Huan peninsula. MacArthur was seventy miles away across the Vitiaz Straits ready to come in and land. Meanwhile, U.S. planes had dropped 1,300 tons of bombs on New Britain in two weeks.

I caught the first two minutes of *Ma Perkins* as I pulled into No-Neck Arnie's, two blocks from the Farraday Building where I had my office.

CHAPTER
2

NO-NECK ARNIE, the mechanic was wiping his hands on a greasy rag when I drove into his garage. Four other cars were there with their hoods open like baby birds waiting for a worm, a bug, or a spark plug.

A radio in the background was playing the Harry James version of "Don't Get Around Much Anymore."

Arnie wore his gray, dirty mechanic's uniform and a look on his face that, as he watched me, said clearly, "You think you've got problems."

Arnie was around sixty, solid with a little belly, blue eyes, and short steel-gray hair. He had no neck or almost none. It would take a trained medical professional to find one if it existed.

Before I got out of the Crosley, Arnie said, "Valves."

Arnie always said, "valves." He seemed to believe faulty, leaky, malicious valves were responsible for all of man's automotive problems. I think if I had asked him what Hitler's problem was, Arnie would have said "valves." He may have been right.

I climbed out and stood next to Arnie as he continued to wipe his hands and look at the car he had sold me about a year earlier, telling me it was a reliable machine that he could keep running.

"It runs on washing machine and refrigerator parts," he had said.

"Does it make ice and clean underwear?" I had asked.

Arnie had grunted and told me the price of the car.

Now he stood before it, walked around it, shook his head. "Looks bad," he said.

"Don't you want to know what the problem is?" I asked.

Harry James hit a high note on his trumpet. Arnie paused to listen and then said, "Valves."

"I get backfire. The car stalls. I think it's sick."

"Leave it," he said reaching out for the keys. I took the car key from the ring and dropped it in his hand. "Give me an hour. Make that two. Scovill is ahead of you. He's got a big problem."

"Valves?" I guessed.

"No, gall bladder. Nice guy."

Harry James held the last note for about eight seconds and I walked out into the morning.

The walk to the Farraday Building took about ten minutes. It was late in the morning as I passed Manny's Taco Palace and looked inside for a familiar face. Manny was the only one I recognized. He looked up from his newspaper behind the counter and nodded. I nodded back and considered a morning taco. I decided to do some work first before rewarding myself with indigestion.

The Farraday Building is on Hoover near Ninth. I don't know who Farraday was, but the building bearing his name deserved to be condemned in 1930 or restored as an historic relic. The owner of the building, Jeremy Butler, poet, ex-wrestler, and friend, lived in the Farraday with his wife, Alice, and their baby, Natasha. Jeremy fought the daily attack on his property with elbow grease, Lysol, and determination.

The Farraday is a refuge for alcoholic doctors, broken-down baby photographers, has-been and never-was movie agents and producers, a fortune-teller named Juanita, a music teacher, and one third-rate dentist named Sheldon Minck whose chamber of horrors was on the sixth floor. I sublet a near closet-sized cubbyhole off of Shelly's chamber.

My footsteps echoed on the fake marble in the dark lobby of the Farraday. There were voices, off-key music, and sounds of machines and typewriters joining the odd beat of my feet. The lobby was wide and six stories high. At each level a black-painted iron railing stood a dozen feet from the office doors. An ancient elevator of the same black-painted iron creaked when I stepped in and whirred slowly upward as I looked down into the lobby. There, Jeremy Butler stepped out of the shadows holding a mop, a bucket, and a bottle of Lysol.

"Toby," he called, growing smaller, which was no mean trick considering Jeremy's bulk. His bald head caught a beam of light from some unseen source. "Thomas Wright Waller died."

"Come again?" I said through the bars as the elevator inched upward.

"Fats Waller," Jeremy said sadly.

"How?" I said, hearing the word echo.

"I don't know," he said. "Died on an eastbound train in

Santa Fe. I think he'd left from here. It was probably his heart. According to the radio, he weighed two hundred and seventy eight pounds, but I've seen him. He was bigger, much bigger."

"I'm sorry," I said.

"I'm writing a poem to his memory," Jeremy said. It was hard to hear him now. I was three floors up and a musical instrument that might have been a trombone hit an ugly note in a nearby office. "It's all I can do."

"Can you stop by?"I called.

"What?"

"Come by my office," I shouted as the elevator vibrated past the fourth floor.

He nodded.

"How are you?" I called, aware of the sorrow in his voice.

"Ain't misbehaving," he said, or at least that's what I thought he said. Jeremy's grammar was always perfect except when he took poetic license.

I finally hit the sixth floor. The door opened and there stood Juanita the fortune-teller. Juanita's real name wasn't Juanita. She came from a good New York Jewish family. She had married a wholesale tie salesman when she was young. He died and she married a mildly successful shirt manufacturer and raised a family. Then husband number two died. Till she was a widow for the second time, Juanita had hidden the fact that she had what she called "the visions." She could tell things about people from touching them or just thinking about them. Sometimes the visions just came unbidden.

Her kids were grown. Her last husband was dead and Juanita had been reborn, so to speak. She had an office in the Farraday and a reasonably healthy business. Most of her clients were Mexicans, with a scattering of Greeks and a dash of Dutch and refugees from the Balkans.

I was convinced Juanita had a real gift, but it carried with it a curse I had experienced on more than one occasion. Whenever Juanita predicted my future, it turned out to be right—but her predictions couldn't be figured out till after the future had come and gone. Jeremy found this particularly interesting. I didn't. Jeremy and Juanita's clients had a better tolerance for her obscure gifts than I did. Usually, I tried to avoid Juanita.

This time I couldn't. She helped me open the elevator door, her beads jangling, her dark long dress dangling. She played the role.

"I had a vision about Harold Stassen," she said.

Stassen, the governor of Minnesota, was a serious contender for the next Republican nomination for president.

"Saw him, clear as I see you now," she said. "In the living room of that mobile home he lives in. His wife was there, one of his kids. He was reading a newspaper. You know what the headline said?"

"No," I answered.

"Stassen will never be president," she said.

"You planning to relay this information to him?"

"Not my business. I'm going down for something to eat," she said. "You want me to bring you something?"

I held the door open for her.

"A couple of tacos from Manny's," I said, reaching into my pocket for my wallet.

"On me," she said. "I'm feeling generous. I just got a big tip from Al Kazinzas."

"Fish Market Al?"

"That's the one," she said with a smile. "I told him he was going to die."

"And he gave you a big tip?" I asked, stepping out of the elevator and letting the door close.

"I said he was going to die at the age of ninety-six in a gondola," she said as the elevator started down. "He said he would stay away from gondolas. But, Toby, if you're meant to go down in a gondola, there's not a goddamn thing you can do about it."

"I'll remember that," I said to her upturned face as she reached the fifth floor.

"Oh God," she said, suddenly remembering something. "Had a vision about you."

"I don't want to hear it, Juanita," I said.

"I'm buying you tacos. You can hear my vision. Okay?"

"Okay."

"You've got ten reasons," she said. "They're all wrong, but you've got to go through them. Like the trials of that Greek."

"Kazinzas?"

"Hercules."

"Hercules with a bad back."

She was almost out of sight below me, but her voice came back.

"The truth will be at the grave."

"Whose?" I called.

"*Ich veis*, who knows?" she said. "I just see this stuff. I don't know what it means. Oh, one more thing. You'll slip on a dead woman."

"What woman? What name? Where?" I asked.

But she was gone.

The sign on the door to our outer office had been changed again. Shelly was forever changing it in the hope of impressing potential and already trapped patients.

This time it read, in gold letters, "Sheldon Minck, D.D.S., V.G.D., Sp.D.I."

Below it in small black letters, a determined client who knew the room number might be able to make out, "Toby Peters, Private Investigator."

When I opened the door a pained voice and a terrible twanging greeted me. My first impression was that it was another of Shelly's victims.

"What are the new initials?" I asked Violet Gonsenelli, who sat behind a tiny desk in the tiny waiting and reception room that had room for only two chairs besides hers.

Violet was dark, young, pretty, and waiting for her husband, a very promising middleweight, to return from the war.

Violet was making a face. The squeal continued.

"The V.G.D. stands for Very Good Dentist. The Sp.D.I. means Specialist in Dental Inventions," she said. "I got a letter."

"Rocky?" I asked, reluctant to open the inner door and see who was in Shelly's dental chair. Rocky was Angelo "Rocky" Gonsenelli, Violet's husband. Violet and Rocky had married four days before Rocky shipped out.

"Yeah, I think he's in the Pacific," she said. "On the *Hornet*. The letter smells like salt water. He says he's fine. Not much else. Says he gets to read the comics. Wash Tubbs is his favorite now. Captain Easy is in Germany helping the resistance."

"I have confidence in Captain Easy and Wash," I said, moving toward the inner door.

"Al Reasoner's fighting Freddie Dawson in Chicago in a couple of days. I'll give you four to one and take Dawson."

I shook my head "no." I had learned my lesson. Don't bet against Violet when it comes to boxing, baseball, or basketball. You had a chance at her in football, but only a slim one.

When I opened the inner door, I was greeted by a sight that would have turned lesser or even greater men to grape juice. Sheldon Minck sat alone in the room in his own dental chair. Short, plump, bald, sweating, and hopelessly myopic, Shelly sat, his ever-present cigar in the corner of his mouth, an intense look on his face. He held a ukulele in his hand and was plucking at the strings and making a sound he mistook for music.

"What are you doing?" I asked before I could stop myself.

"Learning to play the uke," he said. "New idea. Music before drilling and filling. Soothe the patient. Calm my nerves. I'm a passable crooner. No Crosby, or Russ Colombo, Gene Austin, or Rudy Vallee, but not bad."

That was one dentist's prejudiced opinion.

"Can you hold it down for a while?" I asked. "I've got work to do."

"I've got a patient due in a few minutes," he said, getting out of the chair and placing his ukulele on the sink in the corner. "I've almost got 'Hindustan' down."

Down and pleading for mercy, I thought, but I didn't say anything.

"I'm working on a great idea," he said before I could escape. "Articles in *The Journal of the American Dental Association*, *Oral Hygiene*, and *Dental Survey* say Fleers Double Bubble Chewing Gum is good for your teeth, massages the gums, strengthens the teeth."

"Interesting," I said.

"Yeah, strong teeth with cavities from the sugar. But who am I to complain? You know what I mean?"

"I know what you mean," I said.

"So, I come up with a bubblegum with no sugar," he said eagerly. "I sell the idea to Fleers."

"And cut down the number of people who need fillings," I said.

"But what the hell would I care. I'd have a big pile in the bank. I'm working on it. My mind is always working, Toby."

He pointed to the place on his head where he assumed his mind was hidden.

I opened the door to my tiny office, went in, and closed the door behind my desk. Shelly was singing "Ain't She Sweet?" I didn't turn on the lights. The sun was coming in through my single window. I opened the window, turned on my recently purchased secondhand rotating desktop fan, and sat behind my desk.

There were two chairs on the other side of the desk next to the door. On one wall was a photograph of me, my brother Phil, my father in his grocer's apron, and our German shepherd dog, Kaiser Wilhelm. I was about ten. Phil was about fourteen. My father had two more years to live after that picture was taken. My mother had died when I was born, which accounted in part for the permanent scowl on my brother's face.

On the other wall was a large painting of a woman holding a baby in each arm. The woman looked lovingly at one of the babies. There was nothing strange or unusual about the painting and only a few people knew it had been a gift from Salvador Dalí. Two boys in the photo. Two in the painting. A mother in the painting. A father in the photograph. That was the first moment I had noticed the similarities and considered them and the differences.

I pushed my mail to the side after determining that none held the possibility of a check and all held the certainty of a bill. Then I took out my notebook and looked at the numbered items I had written in Chaplin's living room.

The fan hummed. Someone entered Shelly's office. He stopped singing. I could hear him talking now and humming, but I couldn't make out the words.

The unopened mail glared at me. I opened the envelope on top. It was a bill from the telephone company. I put it back on the pile and began to copy my notes. In twenty minutes and an equal number of whimpers from Shelly's patient, I determined that more than half the population of the United States probably didn't care much for Charlie Chaplin. They loved the Tramp, but they hated the man behind him.

My suspects included all anti-Communists, Jews who thought Chaplin had abandoned his roots in a time of Nazi atrocities, Nazi sympathizers and anti-Semites who decided he was a Jew, along with at least eight young women whom he had seduced and abandoned, at least one writer convinced Chaplin had stolen from him, and a bunch of overly zealous Americans who were angry as hell that he hadn't become a citizen. Not to mention Englishmen who thought he had abandoned his native soil, Westbrook Pegler, fans of Eugene O'Neill, and a very wet guy with a very long knife.

"Fiona Sullivan," I said, tapping my dull pencil point on the name that the man at Chaplin's door had spoken. He had given her name and told Chaplin to stay away from her. He had also told Chaplin to abandon his *Lady Killer* project. Why?

There was a knock at my door. I said, "Come in" and Jeremy Butler entered filling the doorway. He had abandoned his mop and Lysol for the visit.

"Edgar Lee Masters has pneumonia," he said solemnly.

"First Fats Waller. Now Edgar Lee Masters," I said.

"He's not dead. You know *Spoon River Anthology*?" Jeremy asked sitting across from me.

"You read part of it to me," I said. "Edgar Lee Masters has pneumonia. Sounds like the start of a good poem."

"Perhaps," said Jeremy, folding his hands in his lap. "You wanted to talk to me."

I told him about my visit with Chaplin and showed him my list. He read it carefully.

"You'd like my help?"

"Can you spare a few days to keep an eye on Chaplin?" I asked.

"I'll consult Alice. She's a great Chaplin fan. As is most of the world."

His wife Alice, formerly Alice Pallice, was always consulted when I asked for Jeremy's help. She never said "no," but she made it clear to me when she could that Jeremy was over sixty with a small child, not to mention a wife. If I ever got Jeremy hurt, I would have to face Alice, and Alice was a formidable figure to face. She was almost as big and strong as Jeremy and two decades younger. She was running a small pornography press in the Farraday when Jeremy had uncovered in her a passion for poetry. Most vivid in my memory was the image described to me by Jeremy of Alice picking up her printing press when the police came one Thursday afternoon. She had gone out the window and up the fire escape with the three hundred pounds of dead weight. Jeremy had covered for her and she had promised to marry him and

abandon pornography for poetry. The two of them published Jeremy's and other people's poetry at a loss, which
was covered by Jeremy's real-estate holdings all over the city.

We went over the list I had made.

"Fiona Sullivan and the warning about making the movie
about the killer are pursuable," he said after a few minutes
of consideration which including touching his ear. "But the
rest is beyond the resources of an entire nation even in
peacetime."

"So . . . ?"

"Search where you have light," he said.

I agreed.

"Shall I go to Chaplin's house if Alice agrees?" he asked.

"If you would," I said.

"I've heard that he's very knowledgeable about poetry."

"Wouldn't surprise me," I said.

"And you'll look for Fiona Sullivan?" he asked.

"Maybe Gunther will be able to spare some time," I said.
"And if things get tough, I might ask Shelly."

Jeremy showed neither approval nor disapproval. He rose.

"I'll let you know in a few minutes," he said as he opened
the door and left.

Shelly was actually singing now. He was much better without the ukulele, but much better only put him in the same
choir as a high-pitched Andy Devine.

I pulled open a deep drawer in my desk and pushed away
broken pencils, rubber bands, paper clips, and a small two-
year-old appointment book I had never used. The telephone
book was in there. I put it on the desk in front of me and
opened it, finding the listings for Sullivan.

It was a start. Fiona Sullivan could be anywhere, but the
wet guy had appeared in front of Chaplin's door in Bel Air

and it made sense that if Chaplin was supposed to stay away from her, she would most likely be close enough so that the warning made sense. But then again, the guy might simply be nuts. He could have picked the name out of the air, a radio show, his own life, or a magazine article.

There were a lot of Sullivans in the Los Angeles telephone directory. Pages of Sullivans. There were three F. Sullivans but no Fionas. I reached for the phone and called the first F. Sullivans.

"My name is Martin Reilly," I said to the woman who answered the phone, using my best Irish accent which, compared to my Italian, Greek, and all-purpose Eastern European, wasn't too bad. "I'm lookin' for a Fiona Sullivan. Might that by any chance be you?"

"My name's Frances," she said.

"That's my misfortune," I said sadly. "You wouldn't be knowin' a Fiona Sullivan, would you now?"

"No," she said. "I gotta run."

She hung up and I went through the next two F. Sullivans. The second was also a Francis, but this Francis was a man. He knew no Fionas. The third F. Sullivan didn't answer. He, she, it, or they were probably at work. I'd try later but I had no great hope.

I looked at the long list in front of me and called the second-floor phone in Mrs. Plaut's Boardinghouse where I had a room. My prayer was that Mrs. Plaut not answer. She was ancient, stick thin, and almost totally deaf.

My prayer was not answered but the phone was—by Mrs. Plaut.

"I'm here," she said.

I took a deep breath. "Mrs. Plaut," I shouted. "It's me. Toby Peters."

"Mr. Peelers is not here," she said. "You can leave him a message."

"No, I'm Mr. Peters," I shouted louder, pointing at my chest as if she could see me over the telephone.

"Good. I've been looking for you this a.m.," she said.

"I've been working."

"Bugs?" she asked.

"No," I said, though I should have said "yes."

Mrs. Plaut was under the impression that I was an exterminator. I do not know where she got this impression. She may have mis-overheard a conversation or misheard a word. When she had an ant problem or a rat problem, she assumed I would take care of it. Somehow, Mrs. Plaut also thought that I was a book editor. The origins of this idea were rooted even deeper into Mrs. Plaut's imagination than the bug theory. And she saw no contradiction or clash between what she saw as my two professions.

Mrs. Plaut had been writing her family history for almost two decades. Every week or so she gave me ten or so neatly printed pages. I paid my rent, took care of her infestations, and read her ever-growing, rambling epic.

"Is Gunther there?" I shouted.

"Mr. Wherthman?" she asked.

"How many Gunthers do you have?" I asked.

"At the moment, only one. I'll get him. Oh, I finished another chapter. I'll put it in your room. Please read it promptly. You took too long last time and I'm getting no younger."

"Which of us is?" I responded, but she had already gone in search of Gunther.

I listened to Shelly humming the Maine fight song (trying for the Rudy Vallee nasal twang), looked at the blades of the fan, flipped the pages of the phone book, and scribbled some names, numbers, and addresses in my notebook while I waited.

"Toby?" came Gunther's voice.

I imagined Gunther standing on his tiptoes and holding his head up to speak into the receiver. Gunther is a midget. Pardon me. He's a little person, a very little person, perfectly proportioned, slim, always well groomed, usually wearing a suit and tie, often with a vest. He slept in a nightshirt.

Gunther lived in the room next to mine at Mrs. Plaut's. He had gotten me to move in more than three years ago after I helped him beat a murder charge.

Gunther was Swiss. He could read and speak a bunch of languages, which was how he made a living. He did translations of books and articles from almost anything into English and occasionally from English into Hungarian or whatever was required. He worked in his room at a normal-sized chair at a normal-sized desk.

"Gunther, how busy are you?"

"Nothing that cannot wait if you have need for my services," he said.

"What do you think of Charlie Chaplin?"

"As a comic actor he brings great humor and pathos to his film roles. I would rank him as a genius. He writes, directs, produces, and stars in his own films and he creates the music. His musical scores are . . ."

"As a man," I said.

"Indiscretion sometimes results from the hubris of the very famous," he said with a sigh. "It happened to the ancients, to great military leaders, musicians, artists, and to actors who believe they will be loved in spite of that which they might say or do. Mr. Chaplin is a victim of such indiscretion in his public utterances and, if the newspapers are to be believed, in his private affairs."

"I'm working for him," I said. "Someone came to his door and threatened to kill him. I've got a few million suspects and one or two leads. The best one is a woman named Fiona Sullivan. I want to find her."

"You would like me to search for her?"

"I would," I said. "You might start with the Los Angeles phone book. There are a lot of Sullivans. I struck out on the first two F. Sullivans. The third doesn't answer."

"You wish me simply to locate a woman named Fiona Sullivan?"

"It may not be simple. If you're lucky, it'll just be boring."

"I will, of course, be pleased to help."

Gunther figured he owed his freedom, maybe his life to me. He had been accused of several murders, particularly the murder of another little person who had been in *The Wizard of Oz* as Gunther had. Gunther hadn't been much of a suspect but he had been handy. He had an accent that sounded German, and he wore a little toothbrush mustache. He looked like a small Adolph or a tiny version of Charlie Chaplin's Tramp if you were feeling charitable. Gunther had shaved off his mustache after he was cleared of the murder charge.

"Great," I said. "Call me in the office if you find her. If I don't hear from you, I'll check in when I get back to the house."

"And so it shall be," he said formally. "Toby, I just finished translating an article for *The Atlantic Monthly*. By a Czech scientist. He says the Nazis are working on a super weapon. He is convinced."

"I'll check it out with Juanita," I said, looking up as the

door opened and Juanita came in with a brown paper bag in her hand. "Talk to you later, Gunther."

"Check what out with Juanita?" she asked, putting the bag down in front of me and sitting.

"You're the fortune-teller," I said, reaching into the bag for a warm, greasy taco.

She put her hands behind her head and looked up at the ceiling while I ate.

"Nothing comes," she said.

"Think big Nazi super weapon," I said, with a mouthful of food.

"Oh, you mean the bomb. Supposed to be a super bomb they'll stick on the front of their rockets and drop on London. They're losing, but they think they'll have us begging when we see the damage."

"What else do you see about it?"

"I don't see anything," she said. "I've got a client, Lars Kirkenbard. You know, the big Dane with the glasses."

I didn't know.

"Well, Lars told me about the bomb," she said. "Everybody knows about the bomb. We're working on one of our own."

"Lars told you?"

"Nope," she said. "I saw it in a vision. Boom, great big explosion, big enough to knock a hole in the ground the size of Zeus's ass. Yeah, he told me. How's the taco?"

"Good," I said. "Thanks."

Juanita closed her eyes. I didn't like it when Juanita closed her eyes. When they opened, she looked straight at me and said,

"Five are gone," she said. "I saw names, five had lines through them. You have a list of names?"

"No," I said, wolfing down my second taco.

"You will," she said, getting up. "I got my Greek waiting. I better go."

I grunted and waved what remained of my second taco and Juanita closed the door behind her. I could hear her say something and Shelly shout and then she was gone. A second or two later Shelly came wobbling through my door, his glasses slipping, a narrow bloody metal instrument in his right hand.

"Did you hear that?" he asked pointing to my door. "That Brooklyn gypsy. You hear what she said?"

"No."

"She told my patient to get out or risk an infection she might not recover from. That's what she said. And my patient pulled off her towel and went out the door. I don't want that woman in these offices again, Toby."

"The patient or Juanita?"

"Juanita," he said. "The patient'll come back. I've got her purse. She never liked me. Juanita."

"You ever work on her teeth?"

"No," he said. "I offered once. She laughed. Then she told me Mildred was going to leave me. And you know what happened."

It wasn't a question. His wife, Mildred, had left him or, more accurately, Mildred had found a good lawyer, kicked Shelly out, and kept everything. Shelly had lived in nearby hotels for a few months and then considered moving into Mrs. Plaut's, a consideration I discouraged. Now he had a two-room apartment a few blocks off Melrose in a four-story courtyard building. It was my opinion that Sheldon was far better off without Mildred, but my opinion was colored by the fact that Mildred hated me. Actually, Mildred hated almost everyone. It was her nature to get mixed up with con men, shady real-estate salesmen, has-been and never-was actors, and almost any man who showed interest in her and could wring her for some of the money Shelly had provided for her.

Shelly did not share my opinion of Mildred, who had bullied, berated, and blasted him since he had married her. Mildred, who reminded me of a cross between Gale Sondergaard and Margaret Hamilton, was the love of Sheldon Minck's life. Losing her had created in Shelly a relentless desire to invent something that would make him millions and bring Mildred back to him.

The phone rang. I picked it up.

"Toby," said Jeremy. "I can give you three days."

"I'll take 'em," I said. "I'll call Chaplin and tell him you're on the way. Thanks, Jeremy."

"I'm going to write the Edgar Lee Masters poem," he said. "Thank you for the idea."

"You're welcome," I said, and gave him Chaplin's address.

He hung up.

"Chaplin has little teeth," said Shelly. "Makes them look bigger when he smiles and shows gum, but they're little. I could do a lot with Chaplin's teeth."

"I'm sure you could," I said, picking up the phone and dialing the number Chaplin had given me.

I let it ring twelve times. A woman answered. I asked her to tell Chaplin that a Mr. Jeremy Butler was on the way from Mr. Peters.

She repeated the message and I hung up.

Shelly showed no signs of moving.

"My stocks are up," he said. "DuPont's at forty-two and a half. GE is at thirty-seven and an eighth and Woolworth has thirty-six and a quarter. Mildred doesn't know about the stock."

"I'm happy for you, Shelly."

"I feel guilty," he said, removing the cigar from his mouth. "Maybe I should tell her."

"Maybe you should," I said. "It'll bring her running back to you."

"You really think so?" he said.

"No. You tell her and she'll get it and give it to . . ."

"I don't want to hear about Donaldo," he said, rising.

"Who's Donaldo?" I asked.

"I don't want to talk about him," Sheldon said, backing to the door, his hand out behind him reaching for the knob. "She wants to be with a . . . a priest, it's her . . . I don't want to talk about it."

"A priest?"

"Well, a reverend, minister. Holy Church of Divine Sublimation in the valley."

"Near your apartment," I said.

"As it happens, coincidentally," he said, opening the door.

"I'd stay with DuPont and Woolworth," I said. "Stay away from Mildred and the ukulele."

He was gone.

I tried the third F. Sullivan in the directory. This time I got an answer. The man said he was Fahid Sullivan. I asked him if he was related to or knew a Fiona Sullivan.

"My real name is Fahid Suliman," he answered in a heavy Turkish accent. "I use the name Sullivan only for my business."

"Which is?"

"I paint signs, store window signs, apartment for rent, dog for sale, and things of that nature. I know no Sullivans."

He asked me if I needed a sign.

One good one from heaven would be nice, I thought, but I said no thanks and hung up. I cleaned stray pieces of taco meat and flour off my desk into the wastebasket, turned off the fan, and headed for the door.

The phone rang. I went back for it.

"Tobias," came Anita's voice. "Potatoes."

"How can I resist?" I asked. "How late will you be there?"

"Seven," she said.

"I'll be there before seven."

"The Roxy's showing *The Fallen Sparrow*," she said.

"I've got a job," I said. "How about Tuesday?"

"You're turning down me and Maureen O'Hara?" she said.

"And John Garfield," I reminded her. "You can't forget John Garfield."

"You're right. I can't," she said with a laugh. "See you later."

I had taken Anita Maloney to our high school prom in Glendale. I hadn't seen or really thought about her in thirty years until a few months earlier. I had run into her where she worked, behind the grill counter at Mack's Pharmacy on Melrose. She had a bad marriage behind her. I had a marriage behind me. We had been listening to each other's stories for a few months.

Working at Mack's, Anita had access to food without the need of ration stamps. When she had more than she needed of something extra for the grill—tomatoes, potatoes, cheese, or hot dogs—she gave me a call so that I could pick it up and bring in tribute to Mrs. Plaut along with my own food stamps. In exchange, she gave me her gas ration coupons.

Shelly was plunking away at his ukulele, his legs crossed, trying to sound like Gene Austin singing "Lady Play Your Mandolin."

"You're getting there, Shel," I said.

"Think so?" he asked brightly.

I nodded. I didn't tell him where I thought he was getting. My guess was somewhere south of a purgatory reserved for people with bad voices who insisted on playing instruments they couldn't control or understand. The next level down was sinners who had to listen to them.

"How can you stand it?" I asked Violet, who was writing out bills.

"I've heard worse," she said with a shrug. "I'll tell you between you and me. Rocky loves to sing. Old songs in Italian. Loves it. But my Rocky can't carry a tune. Can't even drag it across the floor, but does he know it? No. I tell him he sounds like Frank Sinatra. Makes him happy to sing. Makes me happy too. Change of subject. I'll give you six to four on the Maldinado fight next Saturday."

"I'll think about it," I said.

"Offers open till tomorrow," Violet said, sharpening a pencil.

I left. The sixth-floor landing was empty. The sounds from the offices had hit a lull. The elevator was all the way on one. I could walk down before it inched its way up to six. I listened to my footsteps as I went down the stairs.

I had my list of stops to make after I picked up the Crosley from No-Neck Arnie. When I got to the garage, Arnie was standing over the open hood of a Nash, tapping a big wrench in his hand and pondering the fate of the vehicle. If I owned that Nash, I wouldn't have been happy with Arnie's look.

"Am I ready?" I asked.

"Depends," said Arnie, pulled from his reverie. "You talkin' about the bill? That's ready. You talking about will it run? It's ready. You talkin' about the future? That depends."

"On what?" I asked.

"How long I can keep the Crosley going with wire, oil, trial and error, and luck."

"I'm reassured," I said.

"That's what I'm here for," he said looking back at the yawning Nash as he moved toward me. "Sixteen dollars and four cents. Parts and labor."

"What was wrong with it?"

"The water wasn't freezing into ice cubes," he said deadpan.

"That's a Crosley joke," I confirmed.

He nodded and smiled. There were lots of Crosley jokes.

"Valves," he said. "I was right."

I pulled a pair of tens from my wallet and handed them to Arnie, who pocketed his wrench and made change from bills and coins in another pocket.

"How's your son? Hear from him?" I asked, heading for my car where it was parked in a dark corner.

"Got a letter. Says he's fine. Motor pool. Don't know where. Fifth Army."

"I remember."

"It'll be over soon," Arnie said. "Then he's coming back here to work with me again. Jeeps are the future, Peters. Mark my word here. Danny knows Jeeps. Army's gonna sell thousands of 'em when the war's over. We'll put up a big sign, 'We specialize in Jeeps.' "

"I know a guy who can make the sign," I said. "His name's Fahid Sullivan."

"I'll do it myself," he said. "I've got artistic talent."

"Valves," I said, heading for the Crosley.

"Valves," Arnie said. "Oh yeah, I figured out what was wrong with your passenger door. Got a hinge from a Studebaker. It fit. No charge."

"Thanks, Arnie," I said.

"Now, I got a sick Nash," he said, and turned back to his patient.

CHAPTER
3

THE OFFICE OF the Eugene O'Neill Society of Southern California was on Spring Street, a short ride from No-Neck Arnie's. I could have saved rubber and gasoline by calling, but sometimes the best way to get information is to catch someone off guard. Catching Iona Struberki off guard proved unnecessary.

The office was in a one-story strip of six offices, all with doors facing a cracking concrete parking lot. There were five other cars in the lot which provided space for visitors to Hollywood Title and Loan; William Kaar, Attorney at Law; Loyal Friends of Armenia; Arthur Lewis, pet doctor specializing in exotic birds; Jean & Webster Mullicov, profession unlisted; and United Associations of the Arts.

I stepped through the door of United Associations of the Arts and found myself in a small, cluttered office with a small, cluttered desk facing a white-haired woman with a cup of something steaming in one hand and a large cookie in the other.

She smiled up at me as I entered, her right cheek packed chipmunk style. She had clear skin, dark eyes, and a thin nose.

"Can I help you?" she asked, putting down her tea or coffee.

"I hope so," I said. "Miss . . ."

"Iona Struberki," she answered. "Would you like a choco-late-chip cookie?"

She held out a plate. The cookies were large. I took one, looking for someplace to sit. The chair on my side of the desk was piled high with magazines. I stood.

"This is the office of the Eugene O'Neill Society of Southern California?" I asked, taking a bite of the cookie. It was damn good, so I added, "These are great cookies."

"Thank you," she said. "My sister and I made them."

She pointed at the wall to her right. I looked at a line of photographs.

"Third from the right on top," she said. "The one with glasses. That's Mr. O'Neill."

O'Neill, his hair gray, his lips straight, his eyes unfocused looked out at nothing in particular.

"Yes," I said.

"And next to and surrounding him are Lloyd C. Douglas, Louis Bromfield, John Steinbeck, Pearl Buck, John Dos Passos, and . . . but you are interested in our O'Neill Society, Mr. . . ."

"Peters," I said, finishing my cookie. She held out the plate. I took another one. "You have societies for all these people?"

"And many more," Iona Struberki said proudly.

I could smell the coffee now as she took a sip.

"You wish to join? Our Eugene O'Neill Society has a five-dollar-per-year membership fee for which you get two newsletters and the right to attend our monthly meetings of readings from Mr. O'Neill's works. Which is your favorite O'Neill play? Mine is *Desire Under the Elms*. Yours is . . . ?"

"*Strange Interlude*," I said, remembering a scene in a Marx Brothers movie that made fun of the play. I had slept through the Clark Gable movie version of the O'Neill play.

"Esoteric," she said with delight.

"Whenever possible," I said. "How many members are there?"

"In O'Neill? Eighty-six," she said. "I must tell you we are not affiliated with any other of Mr. O'Neill's appreciation groups though we are in contact with many. Not, however, with the so-called Eugene O'Neill Club of the West in San Francisco. You understand?"

"Perfectly. You have a member named Fiona Sullivan?" I asked.

She pursed her lips, put down her cup, and considered the question before raising a finger.

"I don't think so."

She opened a desk drawer, pulled out a ledger book of which the green cloth cover was badly faded, and began thumbing through for her page of O'Neill members.

"No," she said. "Three Sullivans. No Fiona, however. May I ask why you are looking for a Fiona Sullivan and why you expected to find her among our members?"

"Mutual friend, loves O'Neill. Friend and I were talking about Charlie Chaplin and O'Neill's daughter. He mentioned that a Fiona Sullivan was particularly bothered by the marriage."

"Not the only one," Iona said with a sigh. "We were supposed to talk about *Desire Under the Elms* last Tuesday, but we couldn't get past Oona. Very disappointing."

"Sorry I missed that," I said. "Anyone particularly upset, angry with Chaplin?"

This was the time for her to ask who I was and what I wanted, but Iona was caught up in the subject.

"Upset? Almost ended the Society," she said sadly. "I shouldn't be telling a perspective member, but of the fourteen members in attendance, seven staunchly supported the union, seven were appalled."

"Anyone in particular upset?"

"Mr. Kermody," she said, squinting in thought.

"Lean man around forty?" I asked.

"Fat man around seventy," she said. "But full of spunk."

"No lean man around forty?" I pursued.

"You mean upset about the marriage?"

"Yes."

"No. Six women including me sided with Mr. Kermody. Most of our members are older appreciaters of the arts. Most of our members are women. Would you like to join?"

"I want to think about it, talk it over with my friend," I said.

"We'll include free membership in the Friends of Thomas Mann Society," she said. "This month we're discussing the Joseph novels. Wednesday next. There is a good chance Archibald MacLeish will be in town and will attend."

"Tempting," I said. "I'll think about it."

"Meanwhile," she said, holding the plate of cookies out yet again, "might you consider a small donation to our humble efforts for the arts?"

I fished a five from my pocket and handed it to her. She smiled.

"Who's your favorite?" I asked.

She looked at the photographs on the wall, took some magazines and a book from a pile on her desk, and held up a copy of *Random Harvest*.

"James Hilton is my passion. *Good-bye, Mr. Chips* is my favorite and next to my bed at home is *The Story of Dr. Wassell*, which I've just begun. In some ways, I'm a shameless romantic Philistine."

"So am I," I said.

"The war has done that," she said seriously.

I wasn't sure how, but I nodded and left.

The office of the Supporters of the House Un-American Activities Committee was in an office building on First Street not far from Times-Mirror Square. I found a space on the street, almost bumped into a pair of uniformed young Marines looking at a city map, and entered the building. It was neat, clean, and bright with a list of offices behind a sheet of well-polished glass.

The office I was looking for was right on the first floor. Inside the door were four small desks with people, three women and one man, on the phones in front of them. The man was looking at the same nothing as Eugene O'Neill in the photograph, only this man had nothing to see. His eyes were clouded. He was blind. I tried to walk past him to one of the women, but he put down his phone and turned his head in my direction.

"Can I help you?" he asked.

I stopped.

"I'm looking . . . trying to find someone," I said.

" 'Looking' is fine," he said with a small smile. He was

young, dressed in a suit and tie. There was a thick white scar from his hairline to his right eyebrow. "I'm not sensitive."

"Looking for information on Charlie Chaplin," I said, knowing the eyes of the three women on the phones were on me.

"We have some flyers, a short brochure," he said, reaching into a drawer. "I think these are the ones."

He handed them to me.

"Thanks," I said.

"He's a Communist," the blind man said firmly. "He hides behind evasive words, but he is a Red who doesn't hesitate to advocate that American soldiers die for the Russians while he plays golf and grows rich."

"Tennis," I said. "He plays tennis."

The blind man nodded and held out his hand.

"Lucas Rolle," he said.

"Albert Douglas," I lied as we shook.

"As you've no doubt noticed, I'm blind," he said.

"I see."

"I don't," he answered bitterly. "Early in the war, forty-one. Navy. Hawaii. I was on a ship, gunners mate. Last thing I saw was the Pacific Ocean going on forever."

"Sorry," I said.

He nodded.

"I can't see Chaplin movies," he said. "And Chaplin doesn't want to see me."

"You hate him," I said.

"I'm an American," he replied. "And you?"

"I'm an American," I said.

"You want to join our movement?" he asked.

One of the women, short, heavy with large round glasses, had risen from behind her desk and approached us. She could see what Lucas Rolle couldn't hear, that a man was standing in front of him who looked as if he had survived a long series of muggings.

"Need some help here, Luke?" she asked.

"Mr. Douglas is interested in joining us," he said.

She looked at me with suspicion.

"Good," she said.

"He's particularly interested in the Charlie Chaplin situation," the blind man said.

The woman's look of suspicion had turned to distrust.

"You don't like Chaplin?" she asked, staying a safe three feet from me.

"His movies," I said. "His views." Here I shrugged noncommittally. "I want to know more."

"We want him deported," Lucas said.

"We want him tried in court," the woman said.

"And some people probably want him dead," I added.

"If that is your view, I suggest this is not the organization for you, Mr . . . ?" she said.

"Douglas," I supplied.

"We're not in the business of creating martyrs," said Lucas Rolle. "We just want him to go away, to be quiet and go away."

"But there are some . . ." I persisted.

"If you are looking for a violent path," said the woman, "you've taken the wrong first step in coming here."

"Fiona Sullivan sent me," I said.

"Who is Fiona Sullivan?" the woman said.

"She said she was one of your supporters," I said.

"No," said Lucas Rolle. "I don't think so."

"We don't disclose the names or the number of our members but it exceeds two thousand," the woman said. "Luke knows every name. If he says she is not one of us, she isn't."

"I don't understand," I said trying to sound puzzled. "She and this man, thin, about forty, were talking to me at a bar and they sounded ready to lynch Chaplin."

"Then they should be found and stopped," Lucas said. "And if you share their feelings . . ."

"I don't," I said. "I share their indignation but that's it. Is there some group where I might find them?"

Lucas Rolle shook his head sadly. The woman looked at him.

"There are a few but they are hard to find and quite small," the woman said. "And frankly, Mr. Douglas, we would not help you find them even if we could. We are opposed to violence. I lost my husband at Pearl Harbor. I don't want other women to lose their husbands helping Russian Communists. You should also know that I also intend to report this visit to the authorities."

A door opened behind Lucas Rolle and a burly man with a mop of white hair stepped out of an office and stood facing me. He had a folder in his hand. I recognized his face, but couldn't remember his name. He was a U.S. congressman who stood out in a crowd in photographs, a member of the House Un-American Activities Committee. Our eyes met. I turned to leave.

"Peters," he called.

I stopped and turned around. He strode toward me, his hand extended.

"Congressman," I said with a smile, putting my hand into his pulpy grip, trying to remember his name.

"He said his name is Douglas," the woman said.

"Working on something?" the congressman said softly as the chatter went on around him.

"I'm not at liberty to talk about it," I said even more softly.

The congressman put a hand on my arm and nodded knowingly.

"The Rutledge business," he said.

"Maybe," I said, not knowing what he was talking about.

"Our Supreme Court Justice Wiley Rutledge bears watching," he said. "What was it he said a few months ago? 'Democracy is a perpetual compromise.' Peters, we can't compromise where our very existence, the existence of democracy, is at stake. I have an idea. We need more investigators for the Committee. Someone with your knowledge of the film industry could be very valuable."

"Let me get back to you on that," I said.

He nodded and escorted me toward the door. When I was gone, Lucas and the dumpy lady would tell him about my interest in Chaplin. A visit from the F.B.I. might be next.

"You don't remember, do you?" he asked, opening the outer door for me. "Jeremy Butler's, two years ago. A poetry reading in his apartment. I was there with . . . well, never mind."

"You have quite a memory, Congressman," I said.

"And you have a face that's easy to remember," he said with a smile. "I have to run. If I can help . . ."

"I've got it under control," I said.

"You don't happen to recall the poem I read that night at Mr. Butler's," the congressman said, looking back at Lucas Rolle who was on the telephone again.

"No," I said.

"No reason you should," he said. "It was *Song of the Silent* by James Boyd. It ended, 'The crippled boys come back to mule and star. If they shall miss the brotherhood they wanted, our leaders may learn who they are.' Our boys will be heard and our enemies exposed."

He patted my arm and went back through the door, closing it behind him. I was alone in the hall.

I'd made two stops. I had gotten nowhere. I hadn't really expected to make any discovery that would help. My job was to touch all the bases I could find and hope one was right.

I stopped at Mack's on Melrose. Anita was there waiting on a man drinking coffee, looking at a magazine, and worrying the edges of what looked like a toasted cheese sandwich with little nibbles. The man was skinny. A cabby's cap was tilted back on his head.

"Tobias," Anita said, with a grin that didn't hide the fact that she was nearing the end of a seven-hour shift.

I sat at the counter on a red-leather–covered swivel stool and faced her. Anita cleaned up and made up really good, but at work she kept herself clear-faced, efficient, and pleasantly out-of-reach for some of her male regulars.

"Anita," I said. "What do you think of Charlie Chaplin?"

"Funny, sad, says and does dumb things. I really don't think about him much. I'm more the Bob Hope type."

The cabby with the toasted cheese sandwich turned to us and said, "Chaplin's a jerk."

I looked at him. His eyes were on his magazine. He wasn't looking for conversation. He was imparting his version of simple truth.

"I guess that settles it," I said to Anita.

She reached under the counter and came up with a brown paper sack bulging with potatoes. I placed it on the stool next to me.

"Johnny Mack Brown's at the Roxy," I said looking up at the Royal Crown Cola poster behind her. Johnny Mack Brown was wearing a big white cowboy hat, and the quote next to his head said, "I like the best tasting cola of them all." "*The Texas Kid.*"

"First, *The Fallen Sparrow,*" she said.

"Tomorrow," I said. "Maybe the day after. Then how about *The Texas Kid*?"

"And then *Claudia,*" she said.

"*Fallen Sparrow*. Tomorrow night."

"Date," she said, patting my hand. "I'm off early. Pick me up at home?"

"At home," I said.

Something in the way I said it gave me away.

"Ann," she said. "You were thinking about Ann."

I didn't lie.

"I guess," I said.

Ann was my former wife, a contrast to Anita in almost every way. Ann was a full, dark beauty who had lost weight and lost a husband after she left me. Maybe I should explain "lost." Her second husband was dead. Now she was married to a movie actor named Preston Stewart who was still handsome and, after twenty years, still in demand but no longer an A-list leading man. He starred in B programmers with an occasional supporting role at M.G.M. He would pop up in the credits once in a while to remind me of his existence. I had been at their wedding and had to reluctantly admit to myself that I liked the guy.

Anita looked nothing like Ann. She was lean, blonde, and

good-looking, but not a beauty. However, I wasn't looking for beauty, and anyone interested in me wasn't either. We had been doing fine together since I found her here behind Mack's counter less than a year ago.

"Nothing wrong with thinking about her," she said. "God knows I think about my ex more than once in a while. See you tomorrow."

She gave me a smile and a wink and moved to serve two women who had just come in with shopping bags and taken seats at the end of the counter.

Bag of potatoes in my hand, I got out of my car about fifteen minutes later in front of Mrs. Plaut's boardinghouse on Heliotrope. I was home. I walked up the narrow walkway to the porch and went inside. I could smell something inside. It smelled warm, sweet, and a little odd.

"Mrs. Plaut," I called, moving to the open door of her apartment on the first floor.

I could hear her humming inside, deep inside. There was no way she could hear me, but I made the effort louder this time, much louder.

"Mrs. Plaut," I called.

Her bird went crazy, flapping wings and losing feathers inside its cage. Mrs. Plaut kept humming. I took a chance and entered moving toward her kitchen.

I found her wiping her hands on her apron. She sensed that someone was there and turned, a thin ancient figure with a crop of curly white hair.

"Mr. Peelers," she said. "You should knock."

"I did," I shouted.

"Nonetheless," she said. "You should knock. You have . . ."

"Potatoes," I said, handing her the bag.

She took the gift, looked inside, and said, "Potatoes. Good. I'm canning. I'm pickling and canning."

An even dozen jars with "Kerr" written on them stood on the counter near the sink.

"I see," I said.

"Watermelon pickles, fig pickles, chop suey pickles," she said, pointing to one jar filled with a brown substance.

"Chop suey pickles?" I said.

"Cucumbers, onions, green peppers, red peppers, salt, vinegar, water, sugar, celery salt, curry powder. Chop suey pickles. There's a war on, you know."

"I know," I said.

She began putting lids and screw bands on the jars.

"Can't get caps. There's a war on, you know," she repeated.

"It hasn't escaped my attention," I said, knowing she couldn't hear me.

"I have pages for you," she said as she worked. "I'd like you to read them tonight."

She turned to me for confirmation.

I nodded and said, "Tonight."

"You and Mr. Gunther should come for dinner," she said. "Potato surprise. Five o'clock. Miss Simcox and Mr. Bidwell will be joining us."

Simcox and Bidwell were new boarders. Two of the old boarders had married each other and moved out about a month ago. I'd seen little of the new boarders. Simcox was a good-looking, lean woman in her forties who worked in the office at Macy's. According to Mrs. Plaut, Emma Simcox was her grandniece. Mrs. Plaut's natural pallor was morning newspaper white. Miss Simcox was definitely a light-skinned Negro. There was no family resemblance, but Emma Simcox did call Mrs. Plaut "Aunt Irene." Ben Bidwell, on the other hand, was a car salesman at Mad Jack's in Venice. Mr. Bidwell was about fifty, skinny, dark-haired, and one-armed. He had lost the arm at Verdun. Emma Simcox was quiet and shy. Ben Bidwell was either full of optimism and energy, or so depressed he couldn't talk. It promised to be an entertaining dinner.

I checked my watch. I always checked my watch even though it made no sense. It had been my father's. It ran, but what it told me had only a chance relationship to whatever the time might be. I did have a Beech-Nut Gum wall clock in my room that was reasonably accurate.

"We'll be here," I said.

"Vitamin pie for dessert," she said.

I knew I shouldn't ask but I did.

"Vitamin pie?"

"Sent to the Florida Citrus Commission for the recipe. Filled with vitamin C. In the top of a double boiler you mix six tablespoons of cornstarch, four tablespoons of sugar, three-quarters of a cup of corn syrup, a little salt, and you add boiling water, then cook for fifteen minutes. Next you stir it till it thickens and add three beaten egg yolks, cook for another minute and add three-quarters of a cup of canned grapefruit juice and a Number Two can of grapefruit sections. After you pour it in a pastry shell you add more grapefruit sections and cover it with meringue."

"Fascinating," I said. "You'll have to write it out for me."

"It's not for you," she said sternly. "You couldn't cook a can of mush. It's for that sister-in-law of yours. I'll write it all out."

"Thanks," I said. "I'm sure she'll appreciate it."

In the other room, the bird began to screech hysterically.

"The bird," she said. "I have come to the sad conclusion that a strain of idiocy runs in him. I have changed his name."

She had run through five birds since I had been living in her boardinghouse. She changed their names on an almost weekly basis.

"I call him Westinghouse now," she said firmly.

I knew better than to ask why. I simply left the room, got out of her apartment, and climbed the stairs. A small box stood in front of the hall pay phone. It was the box Gunther used to stand on when he made calls. Gunther wasn't in sight. I went to his room. A woman was singing inside in what sounded like German. Her voice was raspy, challenging, and she proudly belted out what sounded like "Mine Berlin." Mining Berlin sounded like a good idea to me.

I knocked.

The woman suddenly stopped singing.

"Come in," Gunther said.

Gunther was seated in the swivel chair at his desk, busily looking at the open phone book and writing something on a pad of paper in front of him.

"One moment," he said, with only the slightest trace of an accent.

I looked around Gunther's neat and comfortable room. A regular-size bed with a dark comforter and big green pillows stood in the corner. There was a low dresser, a small kitchen table covered with a neat, green cloth near the window, a comfortable overstuffed green chair with a reading light and table next to it, and a two-passenger matching love seat across from it. The walls were covered by bookcases that were packed, but neat.

"There," he said with a sigh and turned, pad in his hand.

"I have called the number of forty-seven Sullivans and reached thirty-one of them. None had a Fiona in the household or knew of any Fiona Sullivan with the exception of one Daniel Sullivan who believed he had an old aunt in Cork named Fiona. I shall continue after we dine."

I looked at the clock on his desk where a line of reference books and dictionaries stood against the wall, held in place by matching brass bookends that looked like curious owls.

Gunther reached over to his record player and carefully removed a record. He put it carefully back into the album cover on his desk and looked at me.

"Claire Waldoff," he said, looking at the photograph of the woman on the album cover. "I was playing it a bit too loud perhaps."

"No," I said.

"I confess to having a passion for certain German popular music that predates the current Nazi regime. It is the music of my early youth. Claire Waldoff, Rudi Schuricke, Marlene Dietrich, Zarah Leander, Willi Fritch. I find it best in these times to keep my taste in music to myself."

"I understand. We're expected for dinner with Mrs. Plaut in five minutes," I said.

He looked at the clock.

"Then I shall have to change," he said. "If you will excuse me."

He was dressed in a perfectly matched dark blue suit with a thin red-and-white-striped tie. His white shirt looked as if it had just been ironed, and his shoe shine would have been the envy of General Patton.

"Heard from Gwen?" I asked as he climbed down from the chair.

Gwen was the University of San Francisco graduate student in music whom Gunther had met when we had been on a job more than a year earlier. He had twice mentioned the possibility of marriage. Gwen was pretty, dark, wore glasses, was about fifteen years younger, and a foot and a half taller than my friend. That didn't seem to make any difference to either of them, though the four hundred miles between them did tend to get in the way. Gunther made monthly weekend pilgrimages to San Francisco and everything seemed to be going well. At least, I thought so.

"I have," he said moving to his closet. "She is giving serious consideration to accepting a position with the Boston Symphony."

"Is that good news or bad news?"

"For her, good. For me, bad," he said. "I have been giving serious consideration to moving to Boston."

He looked through his neat row of suits hanging on the low bar in his closet. I didn't want Gunther to move, but I wanted him to be happy.

"I do not think, however, that I will move to Boston," he said, selecting a suit that didn't look particularly different from the one he was wearing. "I will give the situation much thought. Now, if you will excuse me."

He held the hanger with his clean suit in his hand. I nodded, left, and went to my room next door.

Dash, the cat who sometimes hung out with me, had come in through the window I always left open for him. He was blinking up at me from the flowery ancient sofa against the wall, his paws in front of him on the purple pillow on which Mrs. Plaut had stitched, "God Bless Us, Every One." There had been a bed in the room, but I had persuaded Mrs. Plaut to let me store it in her vast garage at the back of the house.

The garage smelled of long-ago livestock and so did every-thing stored in it, but I never planned to use the bed again.

I have a bad back. Actually, it is an evil back that chooses to rebel when I most need it. I could live with the other injuries I had gathered in almost half a century, but I was a slave to my back. I kept a thin, hard mattress rolled up behind the sofa. At night I spread the mattress on the floor and slept on my back. Sometimes Dash joined me.

If Dash didn't wake me in the morning, I could always count on Mrs. Plaut at the stroke of eight. There are no locks in Mrs. Plaut's boardinghouse. She doesn't believe in privacy. There wasn't even an inside lock on the bathroom at the end of the hall. You were expected to listen for signs of human-ity—running water, singing, gargling, toilet flushing—and then you were supposed to knock and enter after a decent pause.

There was a small table near the window to my right. The two wooden chairs at the table matched, sort of. There was also a small refrigerator, toward which I moved in search of something for Dash.

I glanced back at my Beech-Nut wall clock. I had almost four minutes.

There was a leftover burger. I took it out, put it on a plate, and set it on the floor. Dash looked at me from the sofa, then looked at the burger, and turned to stare at something that didn't exist in the corner.

There was no stove in the room. There wasn't enough room even had Mrs. Plaut allowed one, which she didn't. I could have had a hot plate, but I never remembered to pick one up. I took off my jacket, felt my face to see if I needed a shave. I probably did, but I didn't feel up to it.

I thought of Ann and Preston Stewart. As I said, he seemed

like a decent guy for an actor though I heard he had a small drinking problem. That meant nothing much. It went with the job.

Gunther knocked at my door. The knock animated Dash who ambled over to the burger I had put out for him, smelled it, and leapt out of the window in search of his own dinner.

Emma Simcox and Ben Bidwell were already at the table when we said hello and sat down to wait for Mrs. Plaut's arrival. Two pitchers of ice water sat in the center of the table on a white doily.

"He's off again," said Bidwell.

"Who?" I asked.

"F.D.R., war conferences. Twenty thousand miles. You know the total miles traveled since he came aboard as skipper in 1933?"

None of us answered.

"More than 233,400 miles," Bidwell supplied. "And they say the man is sick. Ba-loney."

"No," said Mrs. Plaut, entering with a heavy platter. "Cabbage leaves stuffed with meat-and-vegetable hash."

She placed the platter of fat, rolled-up cabbage leaves in the center of the table and tucked her pink pot holders under her arms.

"I'll get the potato surprise," she said and departed.

Bidwell had leaned over to say something to Emma Simcox.

"I will get back to the phone after dinner," Gunther offered softly.

"I don't think we're going to find her in the phone book," I said.

"But we are not certain," Gunther said.

The cabbage leaves and hash smelled good, and the huge platter of potato surprise was steaming as Mrs. Plaut carried it in. It had little chunks of something dark in the mountain of mashed potatoes.

"What are those?" Bidwell asked, pointing at the potatoes.

"The surprise," Mrs. Plaut said with a smile. "Dig in and remember the starving Armenians."

Mrs. Plaut sat at her regular spot at the end of the table and handed Emma a large serving spoon.

"Our search for Fiona Sullivan is not over," Gunther said, boldly reaching for the potato surprise.

"I hear she is getting married," said Mrs. Plaut, watching the platter of cabbage rolls go round the table and Gunther spoon a modest serving of potato surprise onto his plate.

"Who?" asked Emma.

"Fiona Sullivan," said Mrs. Plaut.

I was holding the platter of cabbage leaves in my hand. Gunther had his first forkful of potato surprise almost to his lips. We looked at each other and then at Mrs. Plaut.

"The surprise is Spam," she said, opening her napkin and putting it in her lap. "Sugar-browned Spam."

CHAPTER

4

"FIONA SULLIVAN?" I repeated.

"Getting married is what I heard," Mrs. Plaut said, holding out two hands to take the platter of cabbage leaves.

"You know her?"

"Who?" asked Bidwell.

"Fiona Sullivan," Mrs. Plaut repeated. "Takes in boarders, too. Used to be in the RKO makeup department, and other places too. Not friendly, but decent enough in appearance."

Where?" I asked.

"Her face, her posture. Some say she's attractive."

"No, where's her boardinghouse?"

Fourteenth," she said. "Fourteenth Place, not Street."

"You have her address?" Gunther asked.

"Of course," said Mrs. Plaut. "You like the surprise?"

"What?"

"Potato surprise," she said.

"Delicious," said Bidwell, who managed amazingly well with one arm.

"Very satisfying," I said.

Mrs. Plaut looked pleased, got up while we ate, disappeared into the other room where Westinghouse went crazy, and returned with a pile of papers, which she plopped next to my plate.

I knew what it was.

"Just leave it in my room. I'll read it tonight," I said.

"Now, I'll bring everyone a cup of cocoa and vitamin pie," Mrs. Plaut answered, pointing to the top of the pile of papers. Written in a neat, penciled script was the name, "Fiona Sullivan," and an address.

For dessert we had the vitamin pie. It wasn't bad. It wasn't good either, but Gunther and I ate it.

"I'll make Cousin Cassie's oatmeal prune cake tomorrow," Mrs. Plaut said. "Your favorite, Mr. Gunther."

Gunther nodded and smiled.

When we were finished, Gunther and I thanked Mrs. Plaut, said good night to Simcox and Bidwell, and hurried off. The manuscript pages and Fiona Sullivan's address and phone number were tucked under my arm.

"Cousin Cassie's oatmeal prune cake?" I whispered to Gunther as we climbed the stairs. "Your favorite."

"I have never heard of this cake before," he said.

Emma Simcox followed right behind us and started past us up the stairs.

"Miss Simcox," I said, "is Mrs. Plaut really your aunt?"

Miss Simcox paused and looked at me.

"Yes," she said. "By marriage. Aunt Irene has told me that she plans to write about our side of the family in her memoirs."

She looked pointedly at the papers under my arm.

"I await that part of her history with great interest," I said.

She moved ahead of us.

It was a little after six. After I dropped the manuscript pages on the table in my room and put the sugar bowl on top of them so Dash wouldn't knock them over, Gunther and I headed for Fourteenth Place. I turned on the radio. It crackled to music and settled into "There's a Small Hotel." When it finished, a baritone voice announced that we were listening to "Claude Thornhill's All Navy Show." Before we reached Fiona Sullivan's we heard Thornhill's renditions of "Portrait of a Guinea Farm" and a jazzy "Buster's Last Stand."

Fiona Sullivan's house was not as old as Mrs. Plaut's and not as big. It was a boxy two-story on a small lot with almost identical houses on either side. There were a few cars on the street, but the houses had small driveways and separate wooden garages that didn't look big enough for anything much larger than my Crosley. We parked and got out.

It had turned dark and cloudy. There were lights on in Fiona Sullivan's. When we stepped closer, I could see that the place needed more than a little work. Dirty white paint was flaking. Beneath the white was a darker color that could have been green.

Some windows were open and I could hear something classical playing inside.

"Schubert," Gunther said. "A bit too melodic for my tastes."

I knocked. The door opened.

The woman who stood there under the porch light was tall, stoop-shouldered, flat-chested, and pale. Her dark hair was tied in a tight bun and she wore round, rimless glasses over narrowed eyes. Her only makeup was a touch of pink in her cheeks that did not become her, and her only touch of near color was a large locket engraved with two silver birds with spread wings that hung from a silver chain around her neck.

"Mrs. Sullivan?" I asked.

"Miss," she corrected, looking down at Gunther, her hand reaching up to touch her silver birds.

"Miss Sullivan, can I ask you a few questions?"

"Why?"

"That is Schubert's *Unfinished*," Gunther said.

She looked down at Gunther.

"Yes."

"A lovely piece," Gunther said. "Schubert himself did not particularly care for it."

"Do you know Charlie Chaplin?" I asked.

"Charlie Chaplin? How the hell would I know Charlie Chaplin?" she asked with a snort.

"Do you know a man about five foot eight, thin hair, maybe wearing glasses, around forty?" I tried.

"Probably no more than fifteen or twenty," she said. "Half the men I know probably look like that."

"We understand you are contemplating marriage," Gunther said. "Congratulations."

"Thanks," Fiona Sullivan answered, but she didn't look particularly happy.

"Something wrong?" I asked.

"Not your business," she said.

"I'm a private investigator," I said, taking out my wallet and fumbling for my frayed license.

She took the wallet, lifted her glasses, and squinted at the license. Then she handed it back.

"How much you charge?"

"Depends on what I'm asked to do."

"Howard's missing," she said. "My fiancé. Come in." We stepped past her and she continued. "You believe in cards, astrology, the like?"

Thinking of Juanita, I said, "There's something to it."

"I don't believe in that stuff. But I believe in fate and your coming to my door when I was thinking about what to do to find Howard, that's fate."

She stepped ahead of us into a living room with dark wooden floors, a faded Navajo carpet, and gray mismatched chairs facing a sofa that strived for gray and came up sun bleached. The walls were lined with black-and-white photographs of women, studio head shots. I looked at them as Fiona Sullivan pointed toward the two chairs.

"I worked on all those ladies," she said proudly as I scanned the wall. "Adele Mara, Mary Beth Hughes, Janis Carter, Ann Dvorak, Helen Walker. And over there. That's Joan Leslie."

"Impressive," I said. "You stopped working."

"Arthritis," she said. "Lost the touch."

"I'm sorry," I said. "Your fiancé . . ."

"Howard Sawyer," she said. "You didn't tell me what you charge."

"Twenty-five dollars a day plus expenses," I said.

She sat, knees together, squinting at me.

"How many days to find him?" she asked.

"I may do this one for nothing," I said. "You made a face when I described a man a few minutes ago. That fit your Mr. Sawyer. Right?"

"What's he done?" she asked. "You want some peanuts and Pepsi?"

"I don't know what he's done," I said. "And peanuts and Pepsi would be fine for me."

She looked at Gunther.

"For me, nothing. Thank you."

Schubert had stopped. Fiona Sullivan got up, moved to a record player in the corner, lifted the playing arm, and turned off the machine. Then she clumped out of the room.

"Charming," Gunther said.

"The night is young," I said.

She was back in the room quickly, holding a glass of Pepsi and a small, half-filled yellow dish of shelled peanuts. She looked around as if she expected something to be missing. Satisfied, she handed me the drink and put the bowl on the small table in front of me next to a pile of *Life* magazines.

"Thanks," I said, taking a sip. The Pepsi was room temperature.

She sat across from me.

"You have many boarders?" I asked.

"At the moment, none. I was renovating. Howard was my only boarder for the past two months."

"No income then?"

"I saved my studio money and came into a tidy enough amount when my mother passed on. What's this got to do with the price of tea in China?"

"Nothing," I said, sipping again.

"So?"

"Mr. Sawyer's room. Did he take his things?"

"I don't believe he has run away," she said. "It's your job to find out what happened to him should I decide to employ you. His room is as it was. His clothes are in the closet and drawers. His desk is untouched. I have changed the linens. Something must have happened to him."

I reached for some peanuts and popped them into my mouth. They were too salty. I crunched and nodded.

"Can we take a look at his room?" I asked.

She scratched her neck, turned her head, and looked at Gunther.

"You're a German," she said.

"Swiss," Gunther corrected.

She shook her head in disbelief. "All right," she said with a sigh of resignation. "Upstairs. First door. Right in front of you. Let's go. I move slow but I'm coming. I climb the stairs as little as I can. Arthritis."

Gunther and I crossed the room with Fiona Sullivan behind us. The stairs were steep, but there weren't many of them. The second-floor landing was narrow, with three doors. I flipped on the lights and moved to the door in front of us. Inside the door I felt for a switch and found it. Two lamps came on.

The room wasn't impressive. It looked a lot like mine at Mrs. Plaut's, only smaller.

"Cozy," I said, looking at the only painting in the room, a large picture of a girl looking down a cliff at the white waves hitting the rocks below her. The tips of the waves seemed to be reaching up for her.

Without a word Gunther moved to the desk. I moved to the drawers. Fiona Sullivan stood watching us, arms folded. I found clothes, period.

Gunther found much more. He stood before the desk, carefully going through papers on top of it and in the drawers.

"Toby," he said, turning to me with a black-and-white composition book in his small hands. The book was open. "At the bottom of the drawer, under stationery and a box of pencils.

"What is it?" Fiona Sullivan asked, moving toward me as Gunther handed me the book.

In neat, black-inked script was a list of names, all women. There were eight names. The first five were crossed out.

"You recognize any of these names?" I asked her.

She squinted over my shoulder.

"Mine," she said.

Her name was number six on the list. The name after hers was Elsie Pultman.

"Any others?"

"No," she said.

"You have friends, relatives you can stay with for a few days?" I asked.

"In Topeka and Abilene," she said. "I'm not leaving my home. Why should I? And come to think of it, why did you come to my door and why are you so interested in Howard Sawyer?"

"Gunther, can you . . . ?"

He knew what I was going to say and answered, "Yes."

"What are you two talking about?" Fiona Sullivan asked.

"Until we find out why there are lines through the names of these five women, I don't think you should be alone," I said.

"You think Howard . . . ? That's ridiculous."

"I shall need some things," Gunther said.

"No," the woman said firmly. "Howard would not hurt me. You have no reason to think he might. You have an active imagination and a wish for my twenty-five dollars a day."

"No charge," I said. "I've got a client."

"You are both confidence men," she said. "A homely confidence man and a tiny confidence man. And I have no confidence in you."

"I've got a contact in the police department," I said. "Let Gunther stay for one night."

She looked at Gunther and said cautiously, "You like Brahms?"

"Passionately," he said, though I was pretty sure he had told me that he didn't like Brahms any more than he liked Schubert. He was strictly a Mozart, Verdi, Bach, and Beethoven fan.

"You want to take a ride with us to Mrs. Plaut's?" I asked.

"Irene Plaut?" she asked.

"Yes," I said. "She said she knows you."

"Conversation with Irene Plaut would drive me mad tonight," she said.

"She had kind words for you too," I said. "I'll wait here while you get some things," I said to Gunther, handing him my car keys.

He had his own car with built-up pedals and cushion, but I knew he could handle the Crosley.

Back in the living room I asked Fiona what she knew about Howard Sawyer. She thought for a few seconds with pursed lips, nodded, and said:

"A gentleman. Came here from Cleveland, tried to join the army but was turned down for medical reasons."

"Medical reasons?"

"He never said what they were. He is a writer."

"What did he write?"

"I don't know. He never showed me."

"His family?"

"All alone in the world," she said with a sigh. "A dear man. I can't believe he's done anything wrong. He's such a gentle man."

And Hitler's a vegetarian, I thought.

I spent the next thirty minutes eating salty peanuts, drinking warm Pepsi, listening to Brahms, and looking at a stack of photographs of B-movie actresses Fiona Sullivan had worked on. My favorites in her collection were Olga San Juan and a very young Wendy Barrie.

"Did men too," she said. "Ron Randell, Steve Brodie, Bob Stack, even Roy Rogers once. He has those Indian eyes. I was the one who figured out how to make them look bigger. I saved careers. Ask June Allyson."

"Fascinating," I said. "May I use your phone?"

"Long distance?"

"No," I said.

"In the hall."

I moved into the hall and found the phone on a table next to the stairs. I fished the number Charlie Chaplin had given me from my notebook and dialed.

"Yes," Chaplin answered.

His voice was steady, almost musical.

"Toby Peters," I said. "I have a lead."

"Excellent," he said. "And I have a problem. Perhaps it would be best if I let your large and engaging associate tell you."

The next voice I heard was Jeremy's.

"Toby," he said calmly. "Someone tried to kill Chaplin."

CHAPTER
5

"WHAT HAPPENED?" I asked, looking at Fiona Sullivan who was examining a peanut between her fingers.

"We were on a covered porch on the second floor," Jeremy said. "We were talking about the British war poets when something came out of the darkness, ripped through the screen, and hit a lamp."

"Something?"

"A knife. Actually a small sword."

"It is an exceptionally large *assigai*," Chaplin said in the background. "A rather dull and unimpressive example of the Indian version of the weapon. I believe it was the weapon my damp visitor had in hand the other night."

"It strikes me as a particularly inefficient attempt to commit murder," Jeremy said. "A heavy, dull knife hurled through a second-floor screen."

"Another warning?"

"Perhaps," said Jeremy.

"We are dealing with a lunatic," I could hear Chaplin say firmly from the background.

"Ask Chaplin if he knows the name Howard Sawyer." Jeremy asked.

"He doesn't," said Jeremy.

"You think you could persuade him to pack a bag and move someplace safe for a few days?"

"I will try."

"Thanks, Jeremy. I think he should stay away from hotels, friends, places he might be recognized."

"You have a place in mind," Jeremy said.

"Mrs. Plaut's. I'll head over there now and prepare her for a new short-term boarder. I think he should give a false name."

"Might she not recognize him?" asked Jeremy.

"Without the mustache, costume, and dark hair? I doubt it. I think I hear Gunther coming back. Convince him, Jeremy."

"I will do my best."

I hung up and turned to Fiona.

"Was that about Howard?" she asked.

"Did he own any knives, swords?"

"Knives? I don't know." She stood up, a palm full of peanuts in her hand.

There was a lot this woman didn't know about the man she had planned to marry.

"One last question," I said, waiting for Gunther's knock. "You said you had some money, this property. Anything else?"

She popped a peanut in her mouth.

"My assets are . . . I am comfortable. You are implying the

71

possibility that my fiancé may have been thinking of marrying me, doing me in, and collecting my small holdings."

"Something like that," I said. "You have life insurance?"

"Both Howard and I have policies," she said. "We are each other's beneficiary. I would have as much reason to want to do him in as he would me, if I were so inclined."

"How big are the policies?"

"One hundred and fifty thousand dollars," she said, "but Howard has a large inheritance."

And that, I thought, was why he was living in a dark Los Angeles boardinghouse with peeling paint.

The knock came.

"The little man?"

"Yes," I said.

She went to answer the door. Gunther entered with a leather suitcase. I looked at the suitcase and he looked at me. I knew there was a small but efficient pistol inside it that Gunther knew how to use.

When I left the two of them and walked back to the Crosley, I could hear music coming from the house. It was classical. It was serious. I was glad I didn't have to stay and listen to it.

There were voices coming from Mrs. Plaut's apartment when I stepped as quietly as I could into the house. It was after eleven. I was drained. A session with Mrs. Plaut might well bring me to tears. I started up the stairs listening to Mrs. Plaut, whose voice carried as far north as Santa Barbara and as far east as the Arizona border.

"It is pure fact, Mr. Voodoo," she said.

"And I believe it," came Charlie Chaplin's voice in answer.

I had reached the stairs. I turned and found myself facing Jeremy Butler.

"Would you like me to return in the morning?" he asked.

"Does anyone else know he's here?"

"No," said Jeremy. "He simply called his wife and told her he was doing research for the movie he was planning."

"*Lady Killer*," I said.

"*Lady Killer*," Jeremy confirmed. "Toby, he is a bitter man."

"Did he complain about coming here?"

"He sighed. I think he welcomed the opportunity to get away from phone calls and reporters."

"And let's not forget lunatic assassins," I said. "I think he is safe here from everything but Mrs. Plaut. Thanks, Jeremy."

"It was interesting," he said. "I finished my Edgar Lee Masters poem. I want to work on it a bit. Perhaps I'll read it to you tomorrow."

"I'm looking forward to it," I said.

"No, I don't believe you are, but exposure to any poetry lightens the soul and touches the mind."

"I can use both," I said.

He nodded and moved slowly out the door and into the night.

I knocked at Mrs. Plaut's door. Westinghouse, her bird, went wild. It sounded as if he were saying something, but I couldn't tell what it was.

"I believe someone is at the door," I heard Chaplin say.

"It's Westinghouse," she said. "The bird. He is given to fits of inexplicable frenzy. It comes from feeding him pine nuts."

"I see," said Chaplin pleasantly, his voice audible over the chattering of the bird. "But someone is knocking at the door."

I heard Mrs. Plaut move across the room to the door pausing to "hush" the squawking animal. Then she opened the door and looked up at me.

"Mr. Peelers," she said. "You should be asleep or reading the very important section I gave you."

"I've had a long day," I said.

"I'm sorry someone gave you the wrong pay, but we must all make it through life in the face of adversity. We have a new roomer. You may come in, say hello, and depart."

She stepped back to let me in, closed the door, and led me to the dining-room table where Charlie Chaplin was sitting with a tea cup in his hand.

"This is Mr. Voodoo," she said.

"Verdon," Chaplin corrected.

"Mr. Voodoo is a bouncer," she explained.

"An announcer," Chaplin corrected patiently.

"I have been telling him that being a bouncer is dangerous work," she said. "Especially for a little fellow like him. He is a little long in the tooth for such work. And he is not getting younger. No one is getting younger. There was talk in my family when I was a young girl that my father's cousin Orton actually got younger when he fell in a vat of tar and almost died, but my mother would have none of it."

"Illuminating," Chaplin said, sipping his tea and beaming at Mrs. Plaut.

"I'm sorry," I said as Mrs. Plaut took a seat across from Chaplin.

"For what? This woman is a nonstop fountain of ideas. And she and her house could well be models for the film I'm working on."

"Mr. Peelers," Mrs. Plaut said, "is an exterminator."

"Really?" said Chaplin with interest.

"And an editor of books," she added.

"A unique combination," Chaplin said with a laugh.

"Howard Sawyer and Fiona Sullivan," I said. "Their names don't ring any bells?"

"None," said Chaplin.

"Elsie Pultman?"

"No," said Chaplin after a moment of thought.

"Jenny Malcom, Elizabeth Gornashuski, May Kelly, Donna Curtain, Zoe Fried?"

"No, I don't believe so," said Chaplin. "What do they have in common?"

"I think they're all dead. I think Howard Sawyer may have killed them. I think maybe Howard Sawyer was the one who knocked at your door."

"Why?" asked Chaplin.

"I don't know," I said.

"Why are you two discussing gardening?" Mrs. Plaut said. "Mr. Voodoo and I were having a delightful conversation about history."

Chaplin crossed his legs and nodded to Mrs. Plaut.

"Mrs. Plaut's great-great-grandfather almost killed George Washington," Chaplin said.

"That's in the pages awaiting you in your room," she said.

"I can't wait to read about it," I said.

"You'll find the tale fascinating," Chaplin said.

"You know," Mrs. Plaut injected, squinting at Chaplin, "you look like someone."

"We all do," Chaplin said with a tolerant smile.

"A person in the moving pictures," she said.

"Thank you," he said, nodding his head and putting his right hand to his chest with a small bow.

Mrs. Plaut pondered. We waited. And then it hit her.

"He has a mustache," she said. "That funny man, Charlie . . ."

I was working fast on an answer.

"Charlie Chase," she said with satisfaction, sitting back. "But he's taller and he doesn't have curly hair. It's brushed straight back. And his face is pinched."

"Then the resemblance is quite superficial if flattering," said Chaplin.

"I'll see you in the morning," I said. "Your room all right?"

"Mrs. Plaut has given me a delightful room," he said.

"With a view, next to Miss Simcox," Mrs. Plaut added. "When the sun comes up, you can see the garage."

"I delight at your landlady's selective hearing," Chaplin said.

"Nobody is getting younger," she said in response.

"With the possible exception of your father's cousin Orton," Chaplin added, holding up a finger.

"An error," she said. "I do intend to write about that incident and bring the truth to light for posterity."

I left with Chaplin leaning attentively toward Mrs. Plaut, who said, "Would you care for some chop suey pickles?"

When I got to my room, I turned on the lights, hung up my clothes in the closet, and changed into a pair of boxer shorts. Mrs. Plaut was certain to burst into my room early in the morning, mop in hand, with questions about the pages she had left for me to read.

Dash was curled up on the sofa, his head resting on the "God Bless Us, Every One" pillow. He looked up at me and went back to sleep.

I put on an undershirt, walked down the hall, showered,

brushed my teeth, shaved with a new Gem razor, and looked at myself in the mirror, brushing back my hair. I needed a haircut. I needed a new nose. I needed a bowl of Wheaties.

When I got back to my room, I poured myself a bowl of Wheaties and milk and a dish of milk for Dash, who walked regally over my mattress on the floor and leaped on the table to join me.

While we ate, I read Mrs. Plaut's latest entry:

My great-great-grandfather Simon was a gentleman farmer in the then colony of Delaware. Some reports have it that he was neither a gentleman nor a farmer but a farmhand who was sent in the place of the farmer to fight for the new United States against the British and their many Indians and Germans and Chinese, mercenaries all with no talents other than killing if we exclude the cooking skills of some of the Chinese.

My great-great-grandfather Simon was given a rifle, an almost new pair of shoes, a knife, and a farewell from my great-great-grandmother Theodora.

Theodora and her six children, four of which belonged to her husband and two of whom, it is believed in the family, bore a more than coincidental resemblance to the farmer.

Simon was gifted with a keen sense of smell, a fine set of teeth, and crossed eyes. Simon met up with the son of a Dover blacksmith named McNally. McNally promised to check up on my great-great-grandmother Theodora if he went back home before Simon, a promise Simon accepted with tears and appreciation and an eventual child who resembled McNally which, by all accounts, was not a good thing because though

McNally was large and strong he looked like a piece of rock.

The near tragedy occurred in the winter. Encamped near the Delaware River, McNally and my great-great-grandfather were night guards while the others slept and snored loudly, some of them passing air. We know of this and the event that followed from McNally's journal which was left to my great-great-grandmother who gave it to her daughter, Mineola, who became my great-grandmother and who misplaced the journal or threw it away considering McNally a man of little honesty and no virtue.

So on that fateful night near the Delaware, Simon and McNally were discoursing quietly on the virtues of rum over other alcohol. Great-great-grandfather Simon was out of sorts having long since exhausted his supply of laudanum.

It was, by McNally's account, Simon who heard the horses coming.

"Hear that?" Simon said.

"Yes."

"It is coming from there," Simon said, looking in two entirely different directions at the same time.

The two Delawarians took aim into the darkness from where there was abundant evidence the sound was coming. The evidence was the smell of horses and men who had not bathed in some time.

"Halt," McNally is reported to have said.

"Identify yourselves," cried my great-great-grandfather.

"It is the party of General Washington," came a voice.

"The password," called Simon.

"There is no password," came the voice which McNally described as either being filled with exasperation or just plain tired, or doing a good job of acting.

"The password is 'Allentown,' " shouted Simon.

"Allentown, then," answered the weary voice.

"I just told you that. So it doesn't count."

"General Washington is tired," the man said. "Let us enter the clearing so you can see our uniforms."

"Anyone can steal uniforms," said Simon.

"We haven't the time for this," came the voice from the dark. "Put up your weapons and let us pass. There is a battle looming tomorrow and the general needs sleep.

"Will one of you please fetch an officer who will provide a modicum of sense to this situation."

With that my great-great-grandfather knew, or thought he knew, that these were not Americans. Americans would not use the word "modicum." My great-great-grandfather was not sure what the word meant but he was certain it was something the British or Chinese would say. And so he fired into the darkness.

The horses in the darkness were displeased and loud and a man groaned. Then shots were fired back at my great-great-grandfather and McNally, who later claimed to have returned the fire.

McNally was hit by a ball in his left leg. He said he took it without a scream. I am convinced that he danced around crying, "It hurts." It was that wound that sent him home early from the war. Well, not home but to Simon's family.

The five or six or seven men on horses came into the clearing.

"You have killed Colonel Pryor," the man on the horse said and indeed an officer was slumped over atop his horse. Next to him rode General George Washington himself.

"What is your name?" General Washington is reported to have said.

"Simon."

"Simon, you have killed a gallant soldier and came near killing me," said Washington trying to keep his horse from going crazy nuts. "You have nearly accomplished what the British have been unable to do."

"It was an error in judgment," my great-great-grandfather said.

"Your eyes are crossed," said Washington.

"From birth," said Simon.

Washington and the dead fellow and the others rode past McNally and my great-great-grandfather. My great-great-grandfather went into a much understandable panic.

"They shall surely kill me," he said.

"My leg hurts," McNally kept saying.

With this my great-great-grandfather threw his rifle into the woods and shouted, "I am heading north to hide in Canada."

McNally claimed that my great-great-grandfather actually had headed west. There is some support for this view. Reports came back to my great-great-grandmother and her kin for more than a dozen years that a cross-eyed wild man in the Ohio territory was occasionally seen quite naked singing something about General, later President, Washington being dead. He was known as Cross-eyed Crazy Joe and became legendary. Sometimes at night in the dark he was heard to change his voice and say, "Your eyes are crossed." There is little doubt that this poor creature was my great-great-grand-father Simon.

The end of this section. Good night.

I cleaned up the bowls, put out the lights, and lay down on my mattress, one pillow behind my head, another next to me to keep me from rolling over. I couldn't sleep on my stomach. The bad back. I had a thin patchwork quilt over me that Mrs. Plaut had made. I heard Dash leap to the window and go out into the cool night.

When I woke it was raining. My Beech-Nut Gum clock on the wall said it was a few minutes after seven. I got up, my back warning me to move slowly. It was too early to call Gunther at Fiona Sullivan's and I didn't know what time Chaplin had gotten to bed.

I could hear the sound of rain on the window. Dash was sitting on my table watching it. It wasn't raining hard but it was enough to keep the sky gray.

I gathered my Kreml shampoo, Dr. West's Miracle-Tuft toothbrush (medium), Pepsodent, and Gem razor, and staggered to the bathroom where I brought myself to some semblance of life. Back in my room I dressed in reasonably clean brown Yank slacks, a definitely clean white shirt with a hole torn low on the tail which I could tuck in and hide, and a dark raincoat. I rolled up my mattress, copied the list of women's names from Howard Sawyer's desk, and wrote a note to Chaplin: "Dear Mr. Voodoo, I'm on the job. Please stay inside. I'll get back to you as soon as I can."

I slid the note under the door of the room Chaplin was in, next to Miss Simcox. Through the curtained window at the end of the landing, I could see the rain coming down gently. Chaplin would wake to its sound and a reasonable view of Mrs. Plaut's garage.

Mrs. Plaut was an early riser. There were times when I was convinced that she didn't sleep, that she stayed up all night writing her family history, searching for recipes, cleaning crevices.

My shoes were in my hand as I tiptoed past Mrs. Plaut's door toward the outside. I came very close to making it this time.

"Mr. Peelers," she said behind me. "Why are you tippy-toeing?"

"Didn't want to wake anyone," I said.

"That makes no sense," she said sternly. She was fully dressed and wearing her blue apron, the one she always wore when she did battle with dust. "I have no cake in the oven. What about my chapter?"

"I left it on my table," I said trying to find the right voice level between letting the boarders sleep and getting through to Mrs. Plaut.

She nodded and said, "And what are your thoughts?"

"Riveting," I said.

She smiled.

"Suggestions?"

"Don't change a word," I said. "Not one word."

"Nothing I can do about the bird," she said sadly. "Westinghouse is a talker. It is all gibberish or Polish or some such like, but it is talking. Where are you going?"

"I think a man murdered five women," I said. "I'm going to try to stop him from killing any more."

"I prefer it when you are not making morbid jokes in bad taste," she said.

"I'm sorry," I answered backing to the door.

"Put on your shoes," she said.

I put on my shoes, but I didn't stop to tie them.

"I'm making eggs mullah for Mr. Voodoo and the others this A.M. in addition to the vitamin pie," she said. "You may stay."

"Can't."

"Extermination or editing?"

"Extermination," I said.

"You should have said so," said Mrs. Plaut. "Meet the day with a smile even though the rain may fall. That is what the Mister said right up to the day he died."

I escaped and stood on the porch for a beat. The rain was a light drizzle. I ran for the Crosley, keys in hand. My brother was probably already in his office. I wanted to catch him before he went out on the street.

On the way I stopped at the Big Round Donut, a shop shaped like a giant donut. I got two coffees and four donuts, three for Phil, one for me.

Armed with this offering in a brown bag, I drove to the Wilshire Avenue police station.

CHAPTER
6

MY BROTHER HAD a small cubicle of an office on the far side of the squad room. I made my way around desks of working cops filing out reports or talking to victims or suspects. Phones rang, typewriters chattered, men and women wept, the guilty proclaimed their innocence as convincingly as if they had been innocent, and the innocent looked as guilty as if they had committed a crime.

One wide-eyed kid with a scraggly beard and no shirt was leaning forward toward a cop who paid no attention to him. The kid was trying to read what the cop was typing. The cop didn't care. He bit his lower lip.

"How do you spell 'orchestra'?" he asked the kid.

None of the cops were young. The young ones were in the army. This was an army of retreads and men who had been persuaded to put off retirement till the war ended. For some of the cops, the war had been a secret gift. They had been scheduled for retirement with no idea of what they were going to do. They couldn't retire to California. They were already here.

My brother, behind the door and through the walls of his small office, could hear every sound in the room I was wading through. He liked it that way. Once he had been promoted to captain and sent across the hall to a big, quiet office. When demotion came, I think he secretly welcomed it.

I stood in front of his office door for a beat. His name was painted on the frosted glass in black letters: Lieutenant Phillip Pevsner.

My name is Toby Peters. As I said, I was born Tobias Leo Pevsner. Just before I became a cop I changed my name to Toby Peters. Why? Less ethnic, easier to remember. That's what I told myself. Now I tell myself other things. Maybe I changed my name to put some distance between me and my past, between me and my brother. My mother had died when I was born. My father had died when I was a kid. I can't remember much about being a kid in Glendale other than that I didn't like it.

My brother never changed his name, never considered it, and didn't like the fact that I had. There was a lot about me that Phil didn't like. He didn't like my work. I had started out as a cop like him, but I had become a studio guard at Warner Brothers and then a private investigator. I had joined the enemy. I had been married. Ann had left me. No kids unless you count me as one, which Ann did. So, I was just passing through, nothing to leave behind.

Phil had a wife, Ruth, and two sons, Nathan and David, and a two-year old daughter, Lucy. Nate was eleven. Dave was thirteen. Phil had a home in North Hollywood. He was a responsible father, a good husband, and he had a steady job.

When I was a kid, Phil had joined the army. He didn't talk much about the war, the war to end all wars, the war now called the First World War. Twenty-three years had passed since he came through the door of our house and took off his uniform for the last time. Two days later he was wearing a blue police uniform. In those twenty-three years, I don't think I ever saw him smile with joy. He was dead serious. I was always a kid. Now, nearing fifty, I still didn't know what I wanted to do when I grew up.

Phil knew what he wanted. He wanted every criminal jailed, crippled, beaten, or run out of town. It was his personal responsibility to do these things. The philosophy was simple, but it had gotten him into a hell of a lot of trouble. For a little over a year he had been a captain in the Los Angeles Police Department, but his heart had been in the streets not behind a desk. His take-no-prisoners approach had gotten him booted back down to lieutenant, which was probably still a notch higher than his temper could handle.

I knocked and he told me to come in.

Phil had a thin stack of stapled papers in his hands. His teeth were clenched. He didn't like what he was reading and when he looked up, he didn't like what he saw.

Phil is about my height, but he is about a foot wider than I am. He's a small tank with steel-white hair cut buzz short. I once said he looked like Ward Bond with a very bad attitude. Phil took it as a compliment.

"Close the door," he said, putting the papers down on his cluttered desk.

I closed the door.

"Sit," he ordered.

I sat at the single chair across from his desk.

"You've got five minutes," he said, checking his watch.

I looked at my father's watch on my wrist. It told me the time was 11:14, which wasn't off by more than three hours. Phil looked at the watch and sat back, his big hands flat on the desk.

"The boys are fine," he said. "Ruth isn't doing all that great. The doctors aren't sure what it is this time. They're working on it. Lucy and the boys would like to see you. So would Ruth. Don't ask me why. That ends family news. State your business and leave."

I took out the list of names and handed it across to him. He took it and looked at it and then at me.

"Fascinating," he said. "Who are they?"

"I think the first five were killed by a man named Howard Sawyer," I said. "I think he's planning to kill the next four."

Phil didn't look impressed.

"I think he moves in with them, takes what they have, and gets rid of them."

He still didn't look impressed. I didn't mention Charlie Chaplin.

"Where did you get this?" he asked.

"Sixth woman on the list, Fiona Sullivan. She's engaged to Sawyer, but he's among the missing."

"You working for her?" Phil asked.

"I'd like to keep her and the others alive," I said.

"You're a saint, Tobias," he said, shaking his head in disbelief. "What's really going on?"

"Just check on those five at the top," I said. "See if they're alive. See if there's a connection. Okay, I'm working for someone else this Sawyer may want to kill."

"May?"

"I think so," I said.

Someone in the squad room went wild with hiccuping laughter. Phil looked toward the door. Crime wasn't funny. He was trying to place the laugh. Was it one of his men? He turned back to the list I had given him.

"You know how long it would take to do this?" he asked calmly. "That's assuming your ladies are dead and were residents of Los Angeles County?"

I shook my head "no."

"If we're lucky, a few hours or days. If we're not so lucky, weeks. If they're not dead, maybe years. And what if they're not from around here? You want me to check with every police department in forty-eight states? The F.B.I.? And what do I say? My brother gave me this list of names. He thinks they were murdered. Five minutes are up."

"No they aren't," I said, looking at my watch.

"How the hell would you know? I'll keep the list, have someone check homicide files. Superficial. I'm not giving this more than an hour of time for a uniform."

"Thanks," I said getting up. "I'll stop by the house next Sunday, see Ruth and the kids."

"Make it Saturday," he said. "I'll be home Sunday."

"Sure," I said.

He put my list aside and picked up the stapled report again. Laughter again from the squad room. Phil took a deep breath, looked at me and then at the door. I left.

Phil was mellowing. As recently as a year ago, I could have reasonably predicted that he would blow up at something I said and throw the nearest heavy item on his desk at me, or even get up and toss me against a wall. But maybe I was mellowing, too. I hadn't said anything that I knew would provoke him. It felt like a truce, with his wife Ruth—thin, pale white— between us, a hand on each of our chests, keeping us apart.

The laughter in the squad room was still audible as I left. It came from a big balding cop talking to a short dark man in his thirties. The suspect had a baffled look on his face. He couldn't figure out what he was saying that was making the cop red-faced and teary-eyed with laughter.

Some things are funny to cops that aren't funny to anyone else. And then there's my brother.

I found a small restaurant not far from the station, went wild and ordered the fifty-cent breakfast (eggs, hash browns, toast, and coffee) and ate while I read the *Times*.

We were winning the war. Slowly, we were winning. The Red Army had jus taken Cherkasy, the last Nazi stronghold on the Dnieper River.

Meanwhile, back at home a sixty-nine-year-old L.A. real-estate dealer had walked into his doctor's office and shot a fifty-four-year-old surgeon twice, killing him. Then the patient had pointed the gun into his own mouth and pulled the trigger. According to the doctor's secretary, the surgeon had removed one of the killer's kidneys. The old man had been convinced the wrong kidney had been removed.

And Amos Alonzo Stagg, now eighty-one and the head football coach at the College of the Pacific, had been named Coach of the Year in the *New York World-Telegram*'s annual poll. Stagg had now been coaching for fifty-three years, forty-two of them at the University of Chicago.

When I finished my toast and paid my bill, I called Fiona Sullivan's number from a phone near the cashier. Two rings and then an answer.

"Sullivan," she answered.

"Peters," I countered. "Everything quiet?"

"Mr. Wherthman is a scholar with excellent taste," she said, a compliment given to those who share one's taste or are assumed to.

"Great," I said. "Nothing from Sawyer?"

"No," she said. "Wait. Mr. Wherthman would like to speak to you."

There was a pause and Gunther came on.

"Toby," he said. "I have made a discovery."

"You like Schubert."

"No," he said, "In Mr. Howard Sawyer's room, a small folder, very small, under the lining of the drawer, under some shirts and sox that needed mending. Actually Miss Sullivan found it while we searched. In the folder are newspaper clippings, five of them, each one dealing with a woman whose name appears on the list you have. All five are dead."

"What do the clippings say?"

"Very odd," Gunther said. "Very odd. One woman fell down a flight of stairs in her own home in Santa Monica. Another in Oxnard was the victim of a hit-and-run driver who was never apprehended. The third in San Diego was a suicide."

"Suicide? How?"

"Poison," he said. "The kind is not specified in the article. The fourth woman who lived in Chicago had a heart attack and the fifth, the fifth was robbed and murdered in New York City."

"Any links?"

"All of the women were over the age of fifty-five. All were widowed or had never married. The oldest, the heart attack one, was eighty years old. There is no time pattern I can determine. All of these deaths occurred in the past two years.

The dates are written in pencil on each clipping. Shall I read them to you?"

I told him to go ahead, and I wrote the names of each woman, the location, the cause of death, and the date of the article in my notebook.

"He might come back for Fiona Sullivan," I said.

"I am aware of this," he said, with a note of determination in his voice.

"Can you stick it out for a while?"

"Yes."

"Thanks, Gunther. I'll rescue you as soon as I can."

"I will look forward to that moment."

I hung up and called Phil.

"The first five women on the list I gave you are definitely dead. I've got the cities they were in and the date of death within a day or two."

"I'm listening," he said.

I read the list to him slowly so he could copy it.

"I'll check when I get a chance," he said. "Anything else?"

"The next name on the list, after Fiona Sullivan, is Elsie Pultman. He might be going after her."

"Might be," Phil said.

"What are you going to do?"

"Check out eleven ongoing felony investigations, meet with the new captain, have lunch, do paperwork. I'll give your information to Josephson. He'll check your list. When I know something I'll let you know."

He hung up.

I went to the phone books, not expecting to get lucky, but I found an E. Pultman listed in Venice. It was worth a try.

The cashier gave me a dollar in change, and I called the Venice number, though given the far-flung locations of the

91

five dead women, I could have been more than three thousand miles off.

The phone rang five times before a woman answered, "Hello."

She didn't sound young.

"Elsie Pultman?"

"Yes."

"My name is Toby Peters. I'm looking for a man named Howard Sawyer."

Long pause and then, "What makes you think I would know anything about a Howard Sawyer?"

"I've got to get in touch with him," I said. "I'm an insurance adjuster. Our company, United Federal National Life Insurance, has a check for Mr. Sawyer in the amount of twenty-two thousand dollars and forty cents. We've been trying to deliver it to him for almost a year."

"Life insurance?"

"His uncle Harold Huber," I said. "If we fail to deliver it within the year, the money will go to Mr. Huber's great niece Cecile in Kansas City. That's Kansas City, Missouri."

The pause was even longer this time and her voice more cautious.

"What makes you think I know where this Mr. Sawyer might be?"

It was a damn good question.

"Your name was in a letter Mr. Sawyer sent to his uncle a short time ago. Obviously, Mr. Sawyer was unaware that his uncle had passed away. Mr. Sawyer had no return address on the letter. We've been searching all over the country for the right Elsie Pultman for several months."

"What did this Mr. Sawyer say about me in this letter?"

"He wrote glowingly," I said.

"Send the check to me and if I ever meet a Mr. Sawyer I'll give it to him."

"Can't do that," I said sadly. "Company policy. I have to deliver it directly into the hands of Mr. Sawyer and he has to sign for it."

"I have never heard of a Howard Sawyer," she insisted.

"Well, I'm in from Baltimore," I said. "I can stop by your home today and leave information for Mr. Sawyer on how he can contact our local office for his check, that is, if you ever run into him or he contacts you."

"I have errands and I don't know any Mr. Sawyer," she said.

"I can be there in less than an hour," I said. "Mr. Sawyer doesn't happen to be there now?"

"No. Not now. Not ever."

She hung up.

I copied her address in my notebook and went out in the drizzle. It was a straight run down Wilshire Boulevard to Venice.

I listened to the Roy Acuff show. Roy sang "Lonesome Me" and "Take Me Back to My Boots and Saddles" and told me to try sweet delicious Meadow Gold butter. "I'll tell 'bout a butter you just can't beat," Roy sang. "The very best butter you can eat. It's Meadow, Meadow, Meadow, Meadow Gold."

The show ended, and, as I approached Venice, I listened to a few minutes of *Big Sister*. The rain was coming down harder. I turned off the radio. I knew something about Venice. Actually, I knew a lot about Venice. Los Angeles history fascinates me partly because so much of southern California, including Venice, was created by con men and eccentrics.

Venice was the brainchild of a world class eccentric named Abbot Kinney. A New Jersey native born in 1850, Kinney served in the U.S. Grant administration. When he left government, Kinney began to manufacture cigarettes. He made millions. Probably addicted to his own product, Kinney developed asthma. To restore his health he moved to southern California.

He fit in beautifully and soon had a reputation as a supporter of odd causes, one of which was the writer Helen Hunt Jackson, author of *Ramona*, which treated the plight of former mission Indians.

But Kinney's vision was big, very big. In 1885 he bought land just south of Santa Monica. He named it Ocean Park and built a resort. Five years later he began work on Venice-of-America. He built a cottage-style development with houses placed along canals and transportation provided by gondolas with little arched bridges crossing the canals. In his desire to duplicate the culture of the original Venice, he screened prospective residents. He had no trouble importing gondoliers, but he had a hell of a time finding buyers who met his expectations. So, he dropped his expectations, but word was getting out that tidal action was flooding the canals.

The experiment was a failure. "Kinney's Folly." Venice went into bankruptcy. The dejected Kinney tried to turn Venice into an amusement park. He built roller-coasters like The Race Thru the Clouds, miniature trains, hot dogs, cotton candy, Hughes Ice Cream Pavilion, and fun houses.

Venice's Grand Canal was filled with concrete and the gondoliers sent back to Italy. Kinney's dream was dead, but Venice lives on. I'd been here as a kid and remembered coming once with my father on the Pacific Electric train and getting off to the noise and crowds at the edge of the Grand Lagoon. We stayed until nighttime to watch the fireworks over the bathing lake and I fell asleep on the ride back to Glendale.

I turned off of Wilshire at eleventh and went south finding my way to Appleby Street where Elsie Pultman's house was in the middle of a row of Victorian-style two-story homes. Hers stood out. It was three stories high, wood, with turrets that made it look like pictures illustrating Nathaniel Hawthorne's *House of Seven Gables*.

I parked and walked up to the door leaving my raincoat in the car. It wasn't raining in Venice. I straightened my shirt, adjusted my belt, brushed back my hair, and knocked.

"Who is it?" came the voice I had heard over the telephone.

"Toby Peters," I said brightly. "I talked to you on the phone less than an hour ago."

She opened the door and looked me over. She was well into her seventies and doing her best to hide the truth. She was thin, arms wrinkled, too much makeup, hair dyed blonde. The result of her efforts was to make her look even older than she probably was.

"May I come in?" I said.

"Where is your briefcase?" she asked. "You're an insurance man. Where is your briefcase?"

"In the car," I said, looking back.

She followed my eyes. The only thing she saw was my Crosley at the curb. She wasn't impressed.

"Let me see the check," she said.

"I can only give it to Mr. Sawyer," I said, with what I hoped was a plea for understanding.

"I'm not asking you for it," she said. "I'm telling you I want to see it."

It was the moment of truth.

"Miss Pultman," I said. "It is Miss not Mrs.?"

"Miss," she said. "I was married briefly in my youth, but I . . . that is none of your concern."

"Howard Sawyer?" I asked.

"Who is this Howard Sawyer?" she said.

"He could be using a different name."

She started to close the door.

"Your life is in danger," I said.

"What?"

"Your life is in danger," I said. "I think your Howard Sawyer has killed five women and is probably planning to kill you."

"You're not an insurance agent," she said.

"No," I said.

"You are a lunatic," she said, fear in her eyes.

"If I could just talk to you for . . ." I said.

She answered me by slamming the door.

"I'm calling the police," she said.

I could do without the Venice police. There wasn't much to back up my story, not yet. I'd wind up having to call my brother, who would not be happy.

"Don't be alone with Sawyer," I called through the closed door. "Or any other thin man about forty and my height."

There was no answer. I went back to the Crosley, climbed in, and sat watching the house, trying to decide what to do. I decided. I went to a public phone booth on Venice beach and called Fiona Sullivan's.

"Peters," I said when she answered. Music was playing in the background. "Can I talk to Gunther?"

"You *may*," she said. "I know you can, but if you're asking my permission, you may."

"You were a schoolteacher," I guessed.

"I was briefly, a long time ago before I discovered that my talent lay in a different direction. Here is Mr. Wherthman."

"Gunther?"

"Toby, everything is quiet here except Mrs. Sullivan and the Victrola."

"Can you talk Mrs. Sullivan into getting out of town for a while?"

"Possibly," he said. "Is it imperative?"

"I think it's a good idea. Take the eight o'clock train to San Francisco at Union Station."

I knew Gunther was familiar with the train. It was the one he took every month to visit Gwen.

"Then," I said, "call Jeremy. See if he can take a few days off. If he can't, call Shelly, tell him to go with you. Sneak out, Gunther. Sawyer may be watching the house. Don't let her leave any notes besides one saying she'll be gone for a few days. I'll call Chaplin. We'll meet you at the station."

"Shall I purchase the five tickets?"

"Please. I'll give you the money when I see you at the station."

"It will be done," Gunther said.

I hung up and called Mrs. Plaut's. When she finally answered, I shouted, "Mrs. Plaut. It's Toby Peters. I have to talk to Mr. Voodoo."

"Who is it?" she asked.

I screamed my message into the phone.

"Why?" she asked.

"Why? I found a book he was looking for. I want to know if I should buy it for him."

"What book?"

"*How to Win Friends and Influence People,*" I said.

"I'll get him."

A few moments later Chaplin said, "Peters?"

"Listen, the guy who came to your door, who threw the knife at you, I think he's killed five women."

"Distressing," he said.

"To say the least."

"Are these women all single, older, living alone?" he asked.

"Yes."

"I see," he said. "Yes. Our damp night visitor is doing what the character I'm writing my screenplay about is doing. He found out about it somehow and is afraid I'm doing research on him. And I am to assume from this that the Fiona Sullivan I was to stay away from is to be his next victim."

"I've got her covered," I said. "On a train out of Union Station for San Francisco at eight. Two friends are going with her. But I think I should get you on that train too and out of town for a while. Meanwhile, there's another woman on our man's list. She won't listen to me."

"San Francisco for a few days is acceptable," Chaplin said. "Though it is a pity I can't spend a bit more time with Mrs. Plaut. She is a treasure trove of ideas. You say this woman, this other woman . . ."

"Elsie Pultman. She has a house in Venice."

"Elsie Pultman," he repeated. "Good name for a character. She won't listen to you?"

"Slammed the door in my face," I said.

"Perhaps I might talk to her. I can, I am told, be persuasive with women."

That I knew from reading the newspapers and listening to Jimmy Fiddler.

"I don't know," I said.

"The man has threatened me," said Chaplin. "I shall have to insist."

"Okay," I said. "I'm in Venice. I'll pick you up in about an hour or so. I don't think we'll have time to get back to Mrs. Plaut's when we finish. We'll head for Union Station. So it will help if you're packed. I don't want to leave Elsie Pultman alone for too long."

"I understand. Then perhaps we should end this conversation."

"Right," I said.

He hung up. So did I. I got in the car, used some of Mrs. Plaut's gas ration stamps, and headed for Hollywood.

CHAPTER
7

WHEN I GOT to Mrs. Plaut's, Chaplin, wearing tan slacks, a white shirt, and a brown sports jacket, was sitting in the living room with his packed suitcase at his side. Mrs. Plaut sat across from him, a jar of something dark in her hand, saying, ". . . most welcome should you ever wish to return, Mr. Voodoo."

Chaplin nodded at me and rose.

"You've been most gracious," he told her taking her hand. "But before I leave I must tell you that I have engaged in a slight deception."

"You are Charlie Chase," she said.

"No, I'm afraid not, but I am Charles Chaplin."

"Carl Kaplan?" she asked. I wondered why there seemed to be a select group of us who Mrs. Plaut failed to hear. "Mr. Kaplan, did you think I would turn you away because you are of the Jewish persuasion?"

"I am not Jewish," Chaplin said patiently.

"Be proud of your heritage," she said. "I am. My ancestors are everything, plus six different tribes of Indian with one Jewish peddler thrown in, I think. Here, this is for you, a jar of sweetbreads and minced tongue."

She handed Chaplin the jar.

"That is most generous of you," he said.

"Cow tongue," she said. "Cow brains. So don't worry."

"I will savor this generous gift," he said tucking the jar under his arm and picking up his suitcase. "Adieu."

Mrs. Plaut smiled, and we went out the door.

"A delightful woman," Chaplin said. "I may return to her for inspiration from time to time."

He held the jar in his lap as we drove.

"This movie Sawyer doesn't want you to make," I said. "He thinks it's about him."

"But it is not," said Chaplin glancing at the jar in his lap. "The idea was given to me by Orson Welles. It is based loosely on the true story of Landru, a Frenchman who murdered a number of women, a worthy inheritor of the name Bluebeard. We are, I fear, dealing with a madman."

"You're probably right, but it doesn't help us much."

The drive back to Venice was slow. The drizzle was back. Afternoon traffic was heavy. Too much time cramped in the Crosley was getting to my back.

Chaplin talked, asked me questions about my work, my background as a cop, and my brother.

"There is a policeman in my movie," he said. "Dogged, determined, in pursuit of my lady killer, a bit like your brother, perhaps."

"Does he catch him?" I asked.

"No, when he catches up to our sympathetic murderer, the

lady killer pours himself a glass of wine fortified with poison. You see, he plans to commit suicide rather than go on trial. The policeman, unaware that the wine is poisoned, takes the drink, downs it in triumph, and dies allowing our protagonist to continue his life of crime."

"Sounds like fun."

"I hope and expect it shall be."

When we hit Venice, Chaplin said, "Not far from here is the location of my first real American film, *Kids' Auto Races in Venice*. That was before I created the Little Fellow. Times were easier then though far less lucrative."

I parked in front of Elsie Pultman's. The drizzle had stopped again. I wished it would make up its mind. Chaplin left his jar of sweetbreads and tongue on the seat, and we walked up to the front door.

The door was open about three inches.

With Chaplin at my side I leaned toward the opening and called, "Miss Pultman."

No sound. I pushed the door open another inch or two and tried,

"Elsie."

Another four or five inches and the door was open. This time I knocked and shouted, "Elsie Pultman."

When nothing happened, I stepped in. Chaplin followed me.

I own a gun, a .38. I seldom carry it. There are many reasons. First, I am a rotten shot. Second, the few times I have taken it with me I've either had it stolen, gotten myself hurt, or messed up a situation that could have been better handled without a weapon. There were two or three times when the gun had saved my life or someone else's, but it was always a gamble. It didn't really matter at the moment. I hadn't even considered taking it from the closet in my room at Mrs. Plaut's.

I kept calling Elsie Pultman's name as we walked through her entryway. A small table with a telephone on it stood next to the stairs leading up. We moved slowly toward the back of the house which was, like Elsie Pultman, overdecorated.

The wallpaper was pink with vertical and elaborate purple designs that looked like chandeliers. The walls in the small living room we walked into were covered with paintings that suggested no common taste or idea. There were old-fashioned forests, hunting dogs, girls filling jugs of water at a fountain, portraits of women with pulled-back hair and lace collars, a bright poster in red with a cartoonlike man with a hammer and something that looked like Russian written under the anvil he was about to strike.

It went on and on. The furniture included a couple of wicker chairs with unmatched cushions, a settee with material that looked like red silk, and a wooden bench with a back about shoulder high that could have come straight from the Folsom Prison resale shop.

"Eclectic," said Chaplin.

We moved further into the house, listening for movement.

In front of the kitchen sink was a poker table covered with the rings left by ancient drinks. At the table were two chairs. Next to the refrigerator on a chipped white porcelain table was another telephone.

It rang. We looked at it and each other and let it ring waiting for Elsie Pultman, if she were upstairs, to pick it up or come running down to answer it.

It kept ringing. I picked it up.

"Hello," I said.

"Put Chaplin on," came a man's voice.

"It's for you," I said, holding out the phone.

Chaplin pointed to himself.

"Me?"

"He asked for you."

Chaplin took the phone, and I ran back in the hall to pick up the phone we had passed.

"Yes," said Chaplin.

"You know who I am?"

"I'm reasonably good at recognizing voices even on the telephone," said Chaplin. "You're the man who, I believe, is generally known as Howard Sawyer."

"That's right."

"And," Chaplin went on, while I tried to stretch the telephone cord far enough so that I could look out the window, "you made an attempt to kill me. It was a very poor effort."

I didn't remember a public phone outside Elsie Pultman's house. I could just get to the door. I kicked it open and looked for one. Nothing there.

"I can do better," the man on the phone said. "I've done better."

"I'm familiar with your list," Chaplin said. "Though I'm convinced at this point that you are insane, I will, for my own satisfaction, tell you that your exploits did not inspire the script on which I am working and that, until you gave me the name, I had never heard of Fiona Sullivan. In short, you are either very stupid, simply insane, or have a great desire to get caught."

"Elsie Pultman isn't there," the man said.

"I see. Where is she?"

"You'll know soon."

"Enlightening," said Chaplin.

"Fiona Sullivan is next," the man said.

"We shall endeavor to keep that from being true. Now, shall we set a time and place to meet? I think you would be a valuable source of information for my project."

"I'm not a fool," he said.

"You are certainly not on the level of Albert Einstein or even Rudolph Hess," Chaplin prodded.

"Leave that house. Go back home. Forget about all this and you live," the man said.

"Ah, I'm afraid it is too late for that," said Chaplin. "I've decided that it necessary to stop you and I will do what is required to attain that end. Now, unless you have something of interest or value to add . . ."

"Peters," the man said. "I know you're listening. You've been looking for me. Now I'm looking for you."

"Then," I said, "we're looking for each other. How about telling me where we can meet and make us both happy."

"Soon," he said.

"Elsie Pultman," Chaplin repeated.

"Number seven. I think I'll be a good citizen now and call the police. You are in Miss Pultman's house without her permission. Imagine the headline: CHAPLIN ARRESTED IN HOME BREAK-IN."

He hung up.

Chaplin came into the hall. We searched the downstairs and the upstairs, closets. No Elsie Pultman.

"What now?" asked Chaplin.

"We've got a train to catch," I said.

"I don't see how running to San Francisco is going to help us find this madman."

"It'll get you and Fiona Sullivan out of town, and maybe, with a little help from the police, I'll find him or he'll find me."

"That plan offers little comfort."

I picked up the phone and dialed. A man came on and gave his name as Sergeant Weitzel. I asked for my brother. He came on quickly.

"Phil, one of the women on that list I gave you is missing. She may be dead."

"Elsie Pultman," Phil said. "She is dead, strangled."

"How . . . ?"

"I got a call," my brother said. "A man told me where to find the body. I sent a car. We found her. Like to know where?"

"Yes," I said.

"In a 1938 Ford, two-door, blue. Car's registered to her. It was and is parked in front of your boarding house."

"Mrs Plaut's?"

"That's where you live," he said evenly. "I think he's sending you a message."

"It looks that way," I agreed. "What now?"

"We find him," said Phil. "We stop him. Maybe he falls down a flight of stairs accidentally before we book him."

"What did you find out about the other five women?" I asked, ignoring the last remark.

"We're working on it. I've got a very bad headache, Tobias. I suggest you get to my office fast."

"Fiona Sullivan's next," I said.

"You're sure?"

"The killer just told me."

"Where is she?" Phil asked. "And where are you?"

"I'm getting her someplace safe," I answered, ignoring his second question.

"That's not your job. You get her killed and . . ."

"You didn't believe me before."

106

"Now I've got a dead woman on your doorstep. Get in here."

"As soon as I can, Phil. Good-bye."

I hung up. The Venice police were probably on the way to the house in which we were standing. In fact, I was surprised that they weren't already here.

"Let's get out of here," I said. "Elsie Pultman's dead."

We went through the front door, down the steps, and got into the Crosley just as the faint sound of police sirens came through the fickle drizzle.

Canned sweetbreads and tongue in his lap, Chaplin looked grim as I urged the car to do its best. We were heading for Union Station.

We hit rush hour and heavy rain and the Crosley sputtered.

"What is that sound?" asked Chaplin.

"Valves," I said.

"It sounds like a fuel mixture problem," said Chaplin.

"You're disputing the word of No-Neck Arnie," I said.

"Forgive me," Chaplin answered. "I would certainly not wish to dispute the word of someone named No-Neck Arnie. You say the train is at eight?"

"Right."

"And," he said looking at his watch, "the current time is 7:10."

I urged the Crosley through the side streets. The rain slowed a little and then a lot. We could hear thunder. I had my foot to the floor, but it didn't persuade the car to make a fresh spurt.

When I saw the station, I said, "Time."

"We have ten minutes, perhaps less," said Chaplin.

We sputtered into the parking lot and got out. It was California hot and humid. Chaplin abandoned his jar and grabbed his suitcase from behind the seat. We made a dash for it. Chaplin was about seven years older than me and twice as fast. I tried to keep up with him. He raced ahead, clearing a path through the crowd, making sudden turns on one foot, a ballet of motion, with me lumbering behind.

As we ran, a crackling voice on the loudspeaker announced without emotion, "Train Number 431 on Track two to San Francisco has been delayed for twenty minutes. Passengers should all be aboard in five minutes. Remember to buy United States War Bonds and Stamps."

I saw Gunther in front of us at the gate and he saw us. He held up the tickets.

"You need not run," Gunther announced. "The train has been delayed. I heard the conductors talking. They are holding departure for someone important."

"This is Charles Chaplin. Mr. Chaplin, my friend and colleague, Gunther Wherthman," I said panting.

"Very pleased to meet you," Chaplin said, taking Gunther's hand.

"My pleasure accompanies my admiration," Gunther answered.

"You've got Fiona Sullivan?" I asked.

"I do," Gunther said, leading the way down the platform.

"Jeremy?"

"He was not available. At your request, I contacted Dr. Minck. He is with Miss Sullivan. I took the liberty of reserving two private compartments, which were fortunately available. We must hurry."

We showed the conductor at the gate our tickets.

We hurried. Gunther climbed onto the fifth car with Chaplin behind him and me in the rear.

"This way," said Gunther.

We followed. Chaplin stopped and turned to me.

"On the platform, just before we boarded the train," he said. "I saw him."

I knew who he meant, but I asked.

"The wet man? Sawyer."

Chaplin nodded and said, "I believe he got on this train. I believe there were two rather large men with him."

"Here," said Gunther. "Compartments six and seven. Dr. Minck is in six."

I opened the door to six. Shelly sat forward, across from Fiona Sullivan who sat erect and as far away as space would allow. Shelly looked up, blinked behind his glasses, and removed his cigar. Had we been a trio of killers, Fiona would be dead before Shelly stood up.

"Keep the door locked, Shel," I said.

"I was prepared," he said, reaching into his pocket and pulling out a shiny round metal bar about six inches long and half an inch around.

"What is that?"

"The bottom half of my new protective essential shield tooth cover inserter, P.E.S.T. The top part . . . let me show you . . ." He started reaching into another pocket.

"Not now, Shel," I said. "This is Charlie Chaplin."

Shelly cocked his head to one side. Fiona Sullivan opened her mouth in disbelief.

Chaplin bowed to Fiona and held out his hand to Shelly, who took it and said, "Nice teeth."

"Thank you," said Chaplin. "I try to observe proper dental hygiene."

"I've got something that'll help," said Shelly. "A rinse. Use it every morning. Tastes like Smith Brothers cherry cough drops. Protects your teeth from everything."

"Sounds intriguing," said Chaplin. "However . . ."

"We're going into the next compartment," I said. "Lock the door. We'll be listening. Don't open the door for anything or anyone including the conductor if you don't hear me with him."

"I'd prefer being with Mr. Wherthman," said Fiona Sullivan with more than a touch of panic in her voice as she looked at Shelly, her fingers moving to touch the two silver birds in flight on her locket.

"I shall be back shortly," Gunther said.

As we closed the door again, I could hear Shelly whisper loudly, "He's shorter than he looks in the movies."

Chaplin, Gunther, and I stood in the corridor for a moment waiting for the sound of the lock. It didn't come. I knocked at the door.

"Who is it?" Shelly asked.

"Lock the door, Shel," I said.

"I was just about to," he answered. "A man can only move so fast."

He locked the door. The three of us went into the next compartment and closed the door.

"The man who's after Fiona Sullivan killed a woman today, the sixth woman on the list," I said.

"Pultman, Elsie," said Gunther.

I nodded.

"He left the body in her car in front of Mrs. Plaut's," I went on.

"Why?" asked Gunther.

Chaplin sat, crossed his knees, and waited for my answer.

"He doesn't like our helping Mr. Chaplin," I explained.

Gunther nodded and said, "Insane. Working in the circus I encountered remarkable people. You," he said looking at

Chaplin, "are familiar with circus people. I saw your film, *The Circus*. You have an understanding of the humiliation and elation of the clown, the mountebank, the person who risks his life more to feel alive and meaningful than to gain money."

"Being in movies is very much like being in the circus," Chaplin said. "But it pays far more."

"I knew a man named Davies, mild, gentle, well read," said Gunther. "One day he rose before dawn and killed four tigers with a crossbow. He didn't harm the lions."

"The tigers had attacked him?" asked Chaplin with interest.

"He was not an animal trainer. He was an contortionist. And there was Klaus Muellenberg with the Royal Danish Circus. A nice man, an aerialist, murdered the Flying Schmidts, all five of them with an antique rifle. Gave no reason. Insanity accounts for much that occurs in the world. One need only read the war news."

It was probably the longest speech I had ever heard from Gunther and I didn't want to interrupt him. But if Chaplin was right, Howard Sawyer and two large men were on the train probably looking for Fiona Sullivan right now. I explained the situation quickly to Gunther and asked, "Any suggestions?"

"We get Miss Sullivan and leave the train," said Chaplin. "Then we seek help from the nearest police officer."

Gunther nodded and I agreed. It was pointless to run to San Francisco if the person you were running from had you trapped on a train.

"Let's go," I said and opened the compartment door.

A very big man filled the doorway. He was wearing gray slacks and a gray polo shirt and a determined, unfriendly look on his bronzed face. His hair was nearly white, but his skin was clear. It was the size of his biceps that most impressed me.

My first thought was, why isn't this guy in the army? My second thought was that there was someone even bigger directly behind him. The bigger man was darker, older, and had a well-trimmed bartender mustache.

"Sit down," the younger one in the door said with an accent that suggested someplace far away and very cold with reindeer. He stepped inside, his partner behind him.

"I think," said Chaplin, "you should get out of our way or we'll be forced to ring for the conductor."

"Sit down," the Viking repeated.

"Please clear the entry," said Gunther, displaying a gun he produced from nowhere.

The Viking looked over his shoulder at the mustached man behind us, then turned back to us and said, "No."

"If you take another step, I will shoot," said Gunther.

"Just let us all sit for five minutes," said the man. "Then we will leave. Which of you is Peters?"

"I am," I said.

"You, we will break your arm before we leave."

"Any particular reason?" I asked.

"We are being paid," he said.

"The guy who paid you is killing a woman in the next compartment," I said.

"If you touch Mr. Peters, I will shoot you," Gunther said.

"I believe he will," Chaplin said.

The Viking shrugged.

"We have already been paid," he said. "We'll break no arm. Just remain where you are. Five minutes."

"We don't have five minutes," I said, stepping in front of him.

"Then," said the Viking, "we shall have to break your arm."

The door to the compartment suddenly opened. The two men in front of me blocked my view. But suddenly there was only one man. Mustache was gone. The Viking turned around and found himself facing Jeremy Butler. He had about twenty-five years on Jeremy but he was outclassed. Jeremy stepped into a bear hug. The Viking pushed his hands against Jeremy's head trying to force him back. Jeremy lifted the younger man off the ground and grunted. The Viking groaned in agony. Jeremy let him drop to the floor.

The man was on his hands and knees trying to get past Jeremy to the now-open door.

"The man who paid you," I said. "Who is he?"

Jeremy blocked the crawling man by stepping in front of the door.

"Don't know," the fallen Viking gasped. "We were at the beach, Venice. Just . . . you broke a rib."

"Yes," said Jeremy.

"The man?" I repeated.

"He gave us fifty dollars each," the man groaned. "And another fifty just before we got on the train."

Jeremy stepped out of the way. The man crawled out and the four of us moved into the corridor. Mustache was staggering toward the end of the car holding his neck in both hands as if he were trying to keep his head from falling off. The Viking was right behind him, trying to stand.

"Alice told me I should come," Jeremy explained, as we moved to the next compartment.

"I'm glad she did," I said, knocking at the door.

"Who is it?" asked Shelly.

"Me, Toby."

"Toby who?"

"Shel, open the door."

"Does someone have a gun or a knife in your back?"

"If they did, could I tell you? Open the door. We have to get off the train."

"Give me a password," Shelly demanded.

"Like what?"

"My receptionist's name."

"Violet."

"Violet what?"

"Gonsenelli," I said.

The lock was pulled back and the door opened. Shelly was alone in the room. The door to the toilet was open. Fiona wasn't inside.

"Where is she?" I asked.

"She needed a Bromo Seltzer," he said. "She went back to the dining car.

"Shelly, I told you . . . forget it."

He joined us in a run through the train, five odd looking men single file providing a free show for the people in the three coaches we passed through. There was no one in the dining car but a few waiters sitting at a table smoking and drinking coffee.

"A woman come in here a few minutes ago?" I asked.

"No," said one of the waiters.

"What's beyond this car?"

"Baggage," said the waiter. "Door's locked. No one came through here."

"She's gone," said Chaplin.

"He has Miss Sullivan," said Gunther.

"She said she needed a Bromo," Shelly nearly whimpered.

Outside the window, a conductor shouted, "All aboard."

"So," said Shelly, "does this mean we're not going to San Francisco?"

I led the procession to the end of the car and pushed open the door. I climbed off with the sound of Shelly's voice behind me saying, "Wait. I've got to get my suitcase."

We didn't wait. There were people on the platform but no Howard Sawyer, no Fiona Sullivan. We ran to the gate and looked around the crowd in the station.

"You see a man and woman just run through here?" I asked the ticket checker. "The woman probably looked scared, about this high."

"Didn't notice such," said the man, adjusting his glasses and looking back at Shelly down the platform waddling toward us.

"What now?" Chaplin asked.

I didn't have the slightest damned idea.

"We go to the police," said Gunther.

"I go to the police," I amended. "Jeremy, you have someplace Mr. Chaplin can stay for a few days? I don't think he should go back to Mrs. Plaut's."

I was thinking about Elsie Pultman in the car on Heliotrope.

"Several vacancies, one furnished on Lankershim, very nice," Jeremy said.

Jeremy had taken a cab. So had Shelly and Gunther. We moved to the cab stand outside the station.

"I nearly forgot," Jeremy said, reaching into his pocket and coming up with a neatly folded sheet of paper. He handed it to me. "Read it when you have time."

"I'm sorry," I said to Chaplin.

"No need to apologize," he said. "I've not had this much excitement since I fell out of the balcony in Manchester when touring with Fred Karno's troupe. Landed on a stout woman who survived and provided me with a look of astonishment I've attempted to duplicate in character actresses ever since. Find Miss Sullivan, Mr. Peters. And stop this lunatic."

They piled into a cab and drove off.

I went back inside the station and made a phone call. Then, I went to my car, drove to the booth, paid my way out, and headed toward my appointment with Phil. I turned on the radio and heard the familiar bonging of a grandfather clock.

Bong . . . "it" . . . *bong* . . . "is" . . . *bong* . . . "later" . . . *bong* . . . "than" . . . *bong* . . . "you" . . . *bong* . . . "think. Lights Out."

I listened to the story about two Nazis who drop into England by parachute to blow something up and find themselves in a castle where they kill their British hosts, who come back to life and act as if nothing has happened. They kill the British again, but they come back. This goes on till one of the Nazis cracks and blows up the place along with himself and his fellow Nazi.

It was heartwarming. Just as it ended I parked in front of the Wilshire Station. Lights out.

CHAPTER
8

THE SQUAD ROOM was almost as busy at night as it was during the day. Actually a lot of criminals like to work a normal day. It makes them feel as if they had a respectable profession like everyone else. Some criminals even have families, wives or husbands and kids. Some.

Phil was in his small office in front of his desk. His tie was loose. He needed a shave and had a cup of coffee in his hand. He looked at me when I walked in and then at the wall in front of him.

"You found Fiona Sullivan's body?" I guessed.

He shook his head, "no."

"Sawyer?"

"No" again.

"What?"

"I'm thinking about retiring," he said, now looking into his cup.

"You? Never."

"I could get a security job," he said. "Regular hours."

"Not you," I said as someone screamed in the squad room. I couldn't tell if it was a man or woman.

"Sometimes I think we're losing the war," Phil said, moving behind his desk.

"We're winning," I said. "Germans and Japs are on the run."

"Not that war," he said. "The war against them."

He nodded toward the door.

"They keep coming. New crop when the old ones get caught or die."

He still hadn't looked at me. His eyes were fixed on the wall across from him. His head was nodding slightly at the truth he had just spoken.

"You won't quit."

"I suppose not," he said. Then he looked up at me. "Ruth won't make it this time."

I sat in the chair across from my brother.

"They said that last time."

"No," he corrected. "Last time they said she *might not* make it. This time it's locked in. Talked to the doctor. Got a second opinion and a third. I'm either quitting or taking time off to be home."

"Starting?"

"Day after tomorrow," he said. "Maybe next week."

I didn't say anything.

"She's an easy woman to live with," he went on. "And I'm a hard man to put up with. I don't think we've had a big disagreement in ten years. She supported Roosevelt. I didn't. She was right."

He held up a pad of paper and took a long slug of coffee. He made a face. It was either bitter or cold or both.

"I made calls about your list," he said. "No Howard Sawyer connected to any of the dead women."

"Pultman," I said.

"She ever tell you she knew him?"

I thought about it. She never had.

"No. But Fiona Sullivan was engaged to him."

"As far as we know, she's not dead."

"Okay," I said. "So Sawyer's not his name. He used different names."

"Why?"

"To get their money."

"No man coming near your Sawyer's description got money from any of the dead women. Three of them just about had a pot to piss in. Only one besides Pultman was murdered, and I talked to the detective in Philadelphia on that one. He's sure it was a murder/robbery. Woman left an estate valued at four hundred dollars to her only daughter. One left what she had, which wasn't all that much either, to a granddaughter who lived with her."

"He made them look natural," I said. "Those women were murdered."

"Why? They have nothing in common that we can find. No relatives. Never met each other. No common interests. Hell, one was a Negro."

"Maybe he's a nut, like in the circus," I said.

"The circus?"

"Never mind," I said. "He has some reason other than money. How much did Elsie Pultman have? Who gets it?"

"That I'll know by tomorrow," said Phil. "There's something you're not telling me, Tobias."

"No."

"Who's your client? Who are you working for on this if it's not the Sullivan woman?"

I could have told him it was Chaplin back when the whole thing started, but now we had at least one clear murder connected to me and, through me to Chaplin. If Chaplin's career was in trouble when I first walked through his door, it would be gone if he got into a scandal like this. Headlines: CHAPLIN MEETS LADY KILLER. CHAPLIN WITNESS IN WIDOW MURDER CASE. WAS KILLER INSPIRED BY CHAPLIN MOVIE PROJECT?

"Can't tell you, Phil," I said.

He nodded again. It was the answer he had expected. I hadn't disappointed him.

"Why did he leave the body in front of your place?"

I could tell Phil's heart wasn't in it. He was going through the motions.

"I'm getting to him, getting close to him. It's a warning. He was going to kill her anyway, so he thought he'd leave a message for me to stop looking for him."

"He's afraid of you." Phil smiled, a smile saying, "That's what I expect from my brother, from the world."

"Something like that."

"It doesn't add up," Phil said.

"I didn't put the numbers down," I said. "He did."

"We'll keep looking for Fiona Sullivan," Phil said.

"If she's dead," I said. There's still one more living woman on the list. Blanche Wiltsey."

"We're looking for her. Any ideas?"

"No," I said, thinking that whoever Blanche Wiltsey was,

she might be dead by now and that would be the end of Sawyer's list and our leads.

"Go," said Phil.

"I'll come by the house on Sunday," I said.

"Do that."

"All right if I bring Anita?"

"Sure," he said swiveling his chair away from me.

"Now what?" I asked.

"I go home," he said. "I go home."

My hand was on the doorknob when he said, almost to himself, "Charlie Chaplin."

I turned. His back was still away from me. I waited for the bomb he was going to drop.

"Charlie Chaplin," I repeated. "Okay. He's my client. Sawyer threatened him, mentioned the movie he's writing about a guy who murders women, gave him Fiona Sullivan's name."

Phil ran his fingers through his bristly hair and looked up at me.

"Didn't I just say Ruth and I haven't had a big disagreement since F.D.R. was first elected? Actually we have one, ongoing. She thinks Chaplin is getting a bad break from the papers and the government. I think he should have his ass kicked out of this country. Ruth thinks he's the funniest man who ever lived. I don't get it."

"Who do you think is funny?" I asked, and I really wanted to know.

"Nobody's funny," he said.

"You know Juanita?"

"The fortune-teller in the Farraday," he said, turning away. "So?"

"She . . . forget it. I'll see you."

I left with my brother's broad back to me and went into the squad room.

A very old man wearing a dark suit with no shirt under the jacket was sitting on the waiting bench across the room.

His eyes were closed and he was rocking back and forth, singing "On the Good Ship Lollipop" in an amazingly good falsetto imitation of Shirley Temple.

I paused at the desk of a detective named Quirst who had lost an eye in World War I and never seemed to be affected by anything that happened around him. Quirst, who was known as Popeye, was looking at the old man. The squad room was about half full now.

"Peters," he said. "You here to cheer up your brother? Or maybe bring him back to life?"

"I'm trying," I said. "What's his story?"

I nodded at the rocking, singing old man on the bench.

"Him? Name's Corkindale. Killed his wife with an iron skillet. Then he killed the family dog, a poodle. Keeps singing and saying 'Lola.' "

"Lola? The dog or the wife?"

"Dog," said Quirst. "World's full of crazies. My philosophy: Don't expect anything good and don't expect people to make sense. Then you won't be disappointed."

The old man on the bench sang, "And there you are. Happy landings on a chocolate bar."

I left.

There were no police cars and no blue Ford in front of Mrs. Plaut's when I got there a little after eleven. I had stopped for a couple of hot dogs and a milk shake at a drug store on Hollywood Boulevard.

I was tired, and I had a prayer: Please God, don't let Mrs. Plaut catch me tonight.

This time God answered my prayer. I took my shoes off at the front door, opened it slowly, and moved cautiously across the entryway, avoiding the familiar spots, which were guaranteed a loud creak. I went up the stairs, expecting that voice behind me. I couldn't face giving a shouted explanation or hearing the tale about Elsie Pultman's body parked outside on Heliotrope.

I made it to my room, flicked on the light, looked at Dash who was on his back next to the refrigerator with his eyes closed. When the light came on, he looked at me, put one paw over his eyes, and went back to sleep.

When I took my coat off, I heard something crinkle in the pocket. I pulled it out. It was the sheet Jeremy had handed me at the cab stand in front of Union Station.

It was a poem with a note above it. The note read: "Here is the poem I told you I was going to write."

It read:

Edgar Lee Masters laying in his bed
returned to the town he had created,
the Spoon River that lived inside his head
where every Miniver and Luke was fated
to seclusion within the mind of the master
who coughed, took his medicine and walked
in his reverie in the moonlit night ever faster
seeing children he had borne and with whom he talked.
"You are me and I am you and we are each other,"
he explains to one man by a mill accident crippled.
"I know," says the man moving slowly in pain.
At the river the poet pauses and looks at a rippled
pool in the water created by a sudden rain.
"Time for your medicine," a hushed voice comes.

Eyes open, he takes a pill. As the nurse softly hums.
Reality it too often seems
comes he thinks to test our dreams.

I put the poem on the table, got undressed, decided to shower and shave in the morning, and lay down on my mattress on the floor after I turned out the light.

The rain was back. Whatever gods there might be couldn't make up their minds. I listened to the sound of the rain pinging against my window. The window was open for Dash, just enough for him to get in or out. It might be raining in. I didn't want to get up to find out.

I felt Dash move next to me, curl against my left side. I touched him and fell asleep.

I dreamed of dead women and a judge who looked like Orson Welles. He sat on a chair above me looking down, his voice echoing in a room about the size of the ballroom at the Hotel Roosevelt.

"What is the connection?"

"They're all dead," I said, craning my neck to look at him.

"So is almost everyone who has set foot on this earth. There is a connection."

Then I realized that there were people behind me. I heard them muttering. I turned to see a tier of basketball bleachers filled with people: Shelly, Jeremy, Mrs. Plaut, Gunther, Chaplin, Anita, Elsie Pultman, Fiona Sullivan, and lots of strange women, all on the older side.

"There is a connection," they said in unison.

Rita Hayworth danced out from behind the bleachers wearing something you could see right through, something billowing and white. She danced around me, the silky costume brushing my face, and she whispered, "There is a connection."

Orson Welles sounded bored when he called down: "Figure it out. Three days and then a decision."

"About what?"

Welles was gone. Dash was seated in his place. Rita Hayworth's silk sleeve gently trailed across my face and a door burst open.

I woke up. Dash's tail was in my face. Mrs. Plaut, broom in one hand, the other on her hip, said: "It is seven in the A.M. and you have a telephone call from Mr. Voodoo."

"Thanks," I said, trying to sit up.

She came in, looked around, and addressed Dash.

"You are not to enter my rooms. You are not to eat any more of my birds."

"He hasn't eaten your birds," I said, getting to my knees. "He isn't interested in your birds. He can make his own way in the world."

"So you say," she said.

"He is a free spirit," I said.

"You'd better talk to Mr. Voodoo," she said. "And then I wish to know if you know anything about the poor woman who died outside my house yesterday."

She bustled in, and I managed to stand.

"Why should I know anything about it?" I asked.

"Because you are an exterminator," she explained.

I checked to be sure my shorts were still on, grabbed a T-shirt from my top drawer, and headed for the telephone on the landing. It was dangling from the cord.

"Peters," I said, feeling my stubbly chin.

"Chaplin," he answered. "I have decided not to hide any

longer. I rejected Mr. Butler's offer of continued sanctuary with proper and sincere appreciation, but I feel it would be somewhat hypocritical of me to hide when I am publicly telling American and Allied forces to face death. I am at home. My wife will return tomorrow. I just spoke to her. She misses me. I certainly miss her."

"I'll send someone to be with you," I said.

"I will not act as if I am under siege," he said. "And I do not wish to alarm my household or my wife when she returns."

"They'll stay outside, in a car. I'll have them introduce themselves and stay out of your way."

"Very well," he said with a sigh of resignation. "Any news about Miss Sullivan?"

"No," I said.

"The police? Are they aware of my involvement in this matter?"

"My brother is," I said. "I had to tell him. But I don't think it will go beyond his office walls unless he needs you to make a statement when we catch Sawyer."

"I understand. I have had a restless night. Something is gnawing at me about this whole affair. Something is odd."

"Something is odd," I agreed.

"I want you to do your utmost to find and protect the last woman on that list you have."

"Blanche Wiltsey," I said.

"Blanche Wiltsey," he repeated. "And I want you to find Howard Sawyer or whoever he really is and bring him to justice."

"I'm working on it," I said, turning to see Gunther emerge from his room, fully dressed in a blue suit with a maroon tie. I nodded. He nodded back.

"Let me know as soon as you have any information."

"I will," I said.

Chaplin hung up. So did I. I turned to Gunther who stood, hands behind his back, waiting.

"There is a connection," I said. "Between Sawyer and all those women."

"Yes," said Gunther. "At least one of which we can be reasonably certain."

"What?" I asked, gauging the distance to my room and then to the bathroom further down the landing. It looked like four or five miles. I wasn't waking up.

"Howard Sawyer is responsible for their deaths," he said. "We must find him. We must ask him. Though by then it will be too late to do anything but satisfy our curiosity. We must recognize, however, the likelihood that he has no motive."

"I've got a call to make, a shower to take, and Mrs. Plaut to talk to. Can you try to track down Blanche Wiltsey?"

"Of course," he said.

"She could be anywhere in the world," I said. "Well, probably anywhere the war isn't going on, which makes the job a little easier, but not much. You have a nickel?"

Gunther reached into the pocket of his pants and came up with the right coin. He handed it to me, nodded, turned, and strode back to his room.

I stood, mouth partly open, one hand on the wall trying to remember the number I wanted to call. I thought I had it. I'm not great with telephone numbers. I can barely remember the one on whichever phone I'm looking at and sometimes not my own at the Farraday, but I thought I remembered this one.

I dropped the nickel and asked the operator to get the number for me. After six rings, a man answered.

"Woodman."

"Al, this is Toby Peters. Did I wake you?"

"Been up for hours," he said. "You get older, you need less sleep, get more reading done, more time to hunt and swim."

"You hunt?"

"Hell no," he said. "What can I do for you?"

Al Woodman was a retired cop, long retired, long widowed. I didn't know how old he was, but it had to be close to seventy. Al was usually up for the odd job when it paid cash.

"I've got some work if you want it. Couple of days. Usual rate."

"What is it?"

"Keep an eye on Charlie Chaplin. There's some nut who may be trying to kill him or just give him trouble."

"I'm in," said Woodman. "When?"

"Now. I'll give you his address. Knock on the door, tell him you're the one I sent, and just sit in the car, keep an eye on the house, maybe look around once in a while."

"I'll need relief. Want me to get Fearaven?"

"He available?"

"I can see," said Woodman. "Hit the bottle when his boy died in Bataan, but he's coming back and he's good."

"Good. Sorry to take you away from the water."

"I hate swimming," he said. "But it keeps me healthy. Anything else?"

"Guy we're talking about has killed six or seven women," I said.

"I understand," Al Woodman said.

Al was short, thin with a Walter Brennan face and sparse white hair. He looked like any other old man, but he wasn't.

Al Woodman had a reputation. He liked guns, all kinds of

guns, all sizes. As a cop he had shot seven people, all justified, though the word was that at least a few of those times he could have shot second and asked questions first. Al had medals. He had a testimonial when he retired. He had a small pension, an aquarium filled with goldfish, and he had very few friends.

I gave him Chaplin's address, told him to call me if anything happened, and hung up.

I made my way back to my room where Mrs. Plaut had rolled up my mattress and was busily sweeping, brushing, and hanging up the clothes I had thrown around the night before. Dash had wisely left through the window.

"No rain today," she said.

"No rain," I agreed gathering my soap, razor, and a towel from my dresser drawer. "You don't happen to know a Blanche Wiltsey?"

Mrs. Plaut paused and blinked at me.

"Yes," she said.

"Who is she?" I asked.

"She? Lance Wilson is a man. Druggist at Schrafts."

"Thanks," I said, moving to the door.

"The dead woman," she said. "The one in the car in front of the house."

I faced her.

"Her name was Elsie Pultman," I said. "She was murdered by a man whose name may or may not be Howard Sawyer. I don't know why she was murdered."

"Too much violence," she said. "On the radio. In the movies. What's his name? Robert Mitchum, the one with the sleepy eyes. Every movie. Shooting. Usually Vincent Price gets shot. Too much violence."

"Then why do you go to movies with Robert Mitchum?" I asked before I could stop myself.

"He looks like my brother Danny's boy, Ephraim," she explained. "Though Ephraim is more stupid looking than sleepy looking."

"I see," I said. "Now if you . . ."

"Ration stamps," she said.

"I'll pick them up today," I promised.

She went back to work singing "The Carioca."

I shaved, showered, brushed my teeth, combed my hair, and returned to my room hoping that Mrs. Plaut had left. She had. Gunther was seated at my table near the window, his feet about four inches from the floor.

"I may have found your Blanche Wiltsey," he said.

"That was fast."

I went to the closet, picked out a shirt that looked reasonably clean, and reached for my Big Yank pants.

"Luck," said Gunther. "A stroke of good fortune. I recalled a Wiltsey Bookstore where I have on occasion located a reference work. It is on Whittier. I called. The proprietor was in early. I asked if he had a relative named Blanche."

"And he does?"

"Yes, a niece."

"Niece? How old is she?" I asked, pulling on my pants.

"I asked that question," Gunther said. "She is twenty years old and about to marry a United States sailor she has known since kindergarten."

"Her family has money?"

"Her father is a plumber."

"She doesn't fit, Gunther," I said. "Profile is all wrong. Name is right, but . . ."

"I called Miss Wiltsey's home. The bookstore owner gave

me the number. A woman, Blanche Wiltsey's mother answered. I said I was looking for a man named Howard Sawyer and wondered if she knew the man. And she said that a person of that name had called yesterday and spoken to Blanche."

"What did he say to her?"

"The mother did not know and the daughter has already departed for work. The mother assumed Sawyer was someone at her daughter's place of employment."

"Where does the girl work?"

I was dressed now and making a decision.

"Coulter's Department store. Music department."

I knew Coulter's. I had passed it twice the day before. It was on the Miracle Mile, Wilshire between La Brea and Fairfax, right next to Citizen's National Trust and Savings Bank, where my former wife Ann and I once had an account. The area was called Miracle Mile by the developers who had bought the land so cheaply and made so much fast money that they had declared it a miracle.

"Shall we go?" asked Gunther.

"Let's do it," I said, going to the shelf in my closet, reaching up behind a battered fedora, and pulling down a cigar box with my .38 inside it.

"Shall I get my weapon?" he asked.

"Why not? If we run into Sawyer, then at least one of us will be able to shoot him."

It was early. Coulter's wouldn't be open for over an hour. We stopped for breakfast at a busy restaurant called William & Mary's, two blocks from the department store.

The place was crowded, the eggs hard, the conversation impossible because of the noise. People ate fast, paid, and ran. We ate slowly and drank coffee.

Just before nine, according to Gunther's watch, we got up and drove to Coulter's. From the parking lot behind the modern, curved-style five-story building, you could enter through a door that opened automatically. We joined the early morning crowd and went looking for the music department.

The store wasn't crowded and finding the music department wasn't hard. Two girls, both about twenty, stood behind the counter of glass cases filled with records. Next to the counter was a stand with a poster on it announcing that Tex Beneke and the Modernaires would be coming in to sign photographs and record jackets of their hit "I've Got a Gal in Kalamazoo." There was a picture of Beneke and the Modernaires on the poster. Beneke had a big toothy grin.

We moved to the first girl, who beamed at us. She was a redhead with short curly hair, freckles, and a well-developed body and smile.

"Can I help you?" she asked, looking at me and then at Gunther. She grinned at Gunther. He smiled back.

"What's big?" I asked.

"You mean what's hot? Vocal? 'Straighten Up and Fly Right,' Nat King Cole. Groovy. 'I've Heard That Song Before,' Helen Forrest. She's also doing great with 'He's My Guy.' Hoggy Charmichael's 'Rockin' Chair.' "

"Classical," said Gunther.

"Longhair? You'll have to talk to Sandra when she comes in."

"Are you Blanche Wiltsey?" Gunther asked.

"Yes," she said, cocking her head to one side. "Why?"

"My name is Peters. This is my associate Mr. Wherthman.

We're investigators." I didn't give her time to ask what kind of investigators we were. "We're trying to find a man named Howard Sawyer. We understand you spoke to him on the phone yesterday."

"Yes, I did."

She should have said "how do you know," but I had the feeling Blanche had a bubbly personality, a good figure, but a poor shot of ever getting on the *Quiz Kids*.

"Mind telling us how you know Sawyer and what he told you?"

"I don't know him," she said. "He told me he'd met me a few weeks ago at a dance. I asked him some questions. He wasn't much for giving information, if you know what I mean. Said he'd like to see me again. I told him I was engaged to a sailor. He said he'd still like to get together. I said I couldn't do that. He wouldn't give up easy. Smitten, I guess."

"You get a lot of that?" I asked.

She beamed.

"I guess. Some. My fiancé says I've got lots of pep. Guys like that. Some guys."

"Where did you leave it with Sawyer?"

"Told him I had to go. He says he has something for me and then he won't bother me again. What've I got to lose? So I say, 'Bring it by the store.' And he says, 'Can't do it. Can I meet him in Pershing Square on my lunch break? So I say it's kind of far and I don't like using the gas. I'm not exactly overpaid. I'm not complaining, but listen, a guy on the phone? You know what I mean?"

"Yes," said Gunther.

Blanche rewarded him with a smile.

"Where in Pershing Square?" I asked.

"Bench under a big palm. Said he'd be the guy in a blue suit with a big white gift box in his lap."

"And?" I prompted.

"Said I'd be there and told him no strings or forget it. He said fine. I don't think I'm going. I just wanted to get off the phone."

The other young woman behind the counter was waiting on a pair of women. The young woman turned and put a record on the player behind her.

"*Bolero*," said Gunther.

"I like it," Blanche said.

"Same passage repeated seventeen times, faster and faster, emphasis on different instruments. A brilliant tour de force."

"It's neat," Blanche said as the music played.

"It's not a good idea to have assignations with strange men in the park or anywhere else," said Gunther.

I think the word "assignations" threw her. She looked at Gunther and said, "Don't I know it?"

"Howard Sawyer is a dangerous man," I said.

"You mean a nut case?" she asked.

"The cashew of nut cases," I said.

"So he doesn't even have a gift for me?"

"Not one you would wish to have," said Gunther as *Bolero* grew louder.

"So, what should I do?" she asked.

"Nothing," I said.

"He'll call me again," she said with a sigh but no sign of fear.

"We don't think you'll ever hear from him again," I said. "But if you do, tell him Mr. Peters will be seeing him and hang up."

"Mr. Peters?"

"Me."

"And what kind of music do you like?" Gunther asked.

"Swing. Goodman, Dorsey, Hawkins," she said.

"I see," said Gunther.

A huge woman with a shopping bag that matched her size stood behind us now, looking at her watch.

"We'll call you at home later," I said to Blanche who beamed at me and Gunther.

The huge woman moved between us and, in a whisper, said to the girl, "What's new from Bing Crosby?"

Gunther and I went back to the car and got in.

"We shall inform the police?" he asked.

"About what? We don't have any witnesses. They're all dead. So they pick up Sawyer. They have no evidence. I don't want to bring Chaplin in and even if I did, all he could say was that Sawyer came to his house and threatened him. No murder charge. I could ask Phil to bring him in, push him around, drop him down a flight of stairs, but I don't think it'd get us anywhere."

"So, what shall we do?"

"We'll have to stop him ourselves."

"And how shall we do that?" asked Gunther as I started the car.

"Oh, lots of ways," I answered, creeping past shoppers in the parking lot. "We could kill him."

"Which you will not do," said Gunther.

"Which I will not do," I agreed. "We can threaten him."

"Which will not work," said Gunther. "And if it did, it would simply drive him off to commit some foul act against humanity elsewhere."

"Which leaves?"

135

"We lay a trap," said Gunther. "Get him to confess his deeds before witnesses."

"Right," I said.

"And how shall we do that?" Gunther asked reasonably.

"I'm working on it," I said. "How much time do we have till noon?"

"A bit over two hours," Gunther said, after checking his vest pocket watch.

"Let's get some help," I said.

CHAPTER
9

THE SUNSHINE WAS gone again. The sky was gray. It looked like rain in Pershing Square but the small park was packed with people on benches eating their lunch out of paper bags, strollers, and servicemen on leave wandering through the city. Plus the regulars.

The regulars were there. Along with those passing out leaflets on everything from the dangers of drinking beer to the need for a wall along the coast to keep the Japanese from landing, they stood on wooden boxes or overturned trash cans. They insulted the crowd or tried to get those gathered around them to accept Jesus, the end of the world, the promise of Communism, the need for universal celibacy, the dangers of Communism, the threat of organized religion, and the necessary preparations for the brave new world coming after the war.

My favorite over the years had been Gibberish Dave who

had come every day for almost two years. Dave had a dark, dirty beard and always wore a ragged suit and a variety of dirt-stained shirts. Dave needed dental work. Shelly had volunteered. I was there. Two years ago.

"I'll take care of your teeth for nothing," Shelly had said. "I've got some experimental procedures I'd like to try. What do you say?"

"I say, I say, I say," Dave had sputtered and spat. "I say refurbishing is not always the answer. The stars hold the answers, but the stars don't speak in words. They speak in codes, blinking. Nazi astronomers understand the code. They're using the code. Notebooks are full of drawings by Leonardo da Vinci and Pope Leopold the Second and Dennis Day. If we don't wake up, we'll all keep sleeping."

"And eating," said Shelly. "But not with those teeth."

"Teeth that bite are bilious," Dave whispered.

"Here's my card," Shelly had said, handing Dave a card. "Come see me."

"Soup and steak?" asked Dave.

"Tuna sandwich and Pepsi," said Shelly.

Dave never took Shelly up on his offer, but week after week, Dave kept coming to Pershing, losing a tooth now and then, making less sense each time I heard him until one day, I began to think I understood him. That's when I stopped listening.

Now we were back in the park, my team deployed, ready, I hoped, for the moment and the murderer.

The meeting we had held an hour earlier in Shelly's office could have gone better. Jeremy stood. Shelly sat in his dental chair slumped forward, head in his hands looking glum and feeling justifiably guilty over the loss of Fiona Sullivan. Gunther sat on Shelly's rolling stool, and I leaned against the door trying to organize.

"Okay," I had said. "You know where to go, which benches to cover, where I'll be. You spot a man with a white box in his lap come and get me. You spot a woman with a white box in her lap come and get me. You spot a trained seal with a box in its lap come and get me. Don't grab the person with the box. We do that together."

"You don't need me," said Shelly, moving his cigar to the other side of his mouth. "I'll mess it up. I got Fiona Sullivan killed. I'll get someone else killed. Let's face it. I'm not a detective. I'm a dentist."

His conclusion was debatable, but I didn't have the time.

"We need you," I said.

"Call in the police," he grumbled.

"I told you why we couldn't," I said.

"We need your help, Dr. Minck," Gunther said solemnly.

I don't think Jeremy was so sure about Shelly's potential contribution, but he said, "Sheldon, rise above your guilt."

Shelly shook his head and sighed deeply.

"All right," he said.

Gunther and I had guns, but neither of us planned to use them for anything other than pointing at Sawyer. The likely result of my firing at any target in Pershing Square would be the death or wounding of relatively innocent bystanders. Gunther would probably hit him, but without evidence the little man would find himself up on an assault or murder charge.

The idea was simple. Hide as well as we could—which was not easy for this quartet, especially Gunther and Jeremy—and then converge on Sawyer when he was spotted.

Surround him, bring him in. Get him to talk. Hope for the best. One of my better plans.

We separated. I joined a group gathered around a malnourished skeleton of man standing on a rock. His bony arms jutted out of his too-short jacket, and his voice rattled as he waved his arms in the air and told the crowd:

"Money is corruption. Barter is salvation. Work for your daily bread, not the money to buy your daily bread, for as sure as the rain will come, someone will gather your coins, your dollars, and buy *you*. Look at yourselves. You're already bought. Throw your money away and be free. Look."

He emptied his pockets. Nothing but lint.

People drifted away. The crowd was small. I tried to hide inside it while keeping an eye on three benches. There were people sitting on them, but none with white boxes and none that looked like Chaplin's description of Sawyer.

I drifted out of the crowd and moved toward Gunther's benches. I couldn't see him, but I was sure he was there, probably behind a tree.

Jeremy was standing right in front of a man on a wooden box, a fat man with a red nose who was telling the amused men and women that touching even one drop of alcohol was the same as turning one's soul over to the devil.

The trouble started when I moved toward Shelly's two benches. I didn't see him. I didn't see anyone on the benches who might be Sawyer. And then I heard it, Shelly's voice in the bushes.

"No," he whined.

I ran in the direction of his voice pushing through a group of sailors, running around some high bushes. I found Shelly facing a policeman, a grizzled older guy in uniform holding a billy club.

"I'm not doing anything wrong," Shelly said.

"You're hiding in the bushes. What are you doin' hiding in the bushes?"

"I'm a dentist," Shelly explained, adjusting his glasses.

"You were looking at those kids."

"No," Shelly said. "I . . . Toby, tell him."

The cop turned to me, warily.

"He's a dentist," I confirmed.

"And what the hell's that got to do with anything?" asked the cop. "I've seen perverts in this park who were brain surgeons, congressmen, and army colonels."

"I lost a gold filling back here this morning," I said. "Dr. Minck came to help me find it."

"Special filling," said Shelly. "Experimental. Very valuable. Must find it."

"And what," asked the cop, "were you doin' back here when you lost your fillin'?"

"I confess," I said. "I was . . . you know."

"Pissing in the park," the cop said.

Now I placed him. He looked like Edgar Kennedy about to do his famous slow burn.

"I couldn't wait," I said. "Weak bladder."

That was the moment Gunther came running through the bushes toward us saying, "Man with a white box on his lap. This way."

"Who the devil are you?" asked the cop. "What the hell is this about a white box?"

"We think the man with the white box has my filling," I said. "Someone saw a man with a white box back here a little while ago."

"I think we should all take a walk to the call box and call for a ride to the station," he said.

The cop was facing me and Gunther, his back to Shelly. Shelly rushed forward, bumped into the cop, and sent him forward on his face.

"Go," shouted Shelly, whose glasses had flown off. "Get him. Leave me. Save yourself."

He had the overdramatic quiver of bad actor delivering a cliché with all that he could give to it. Gunther and I ran through the bushes, into the crowd, and along the walk.

"There," said Gunther.

There were three people on the bench. A soldier in uniform with his cap tilted back and a young girl holding his arm were feeding peanuts to a squirrel. Next to them sat a fat young man with a large white box in his lap. The fat man was biting his lower lip.

"It's not him," I said.

"But he has a box. Perhaps he is the accomplice of this murderer?"

The fat man who wore fat pants and a fat sweater kept one hand on the box and the other hand busy mopping his brow.

"Sawyer may be watching," I said.

We looked around. There was no one who resembled Sawyer, but he might be wearing some kind of disguise. He could be a hundred feet away in the trees with binoculars.

The fat man sat.

"Let's ask him," I finally said.

We moved forward toward the man who saw us approaching. He seemed especially interested in Gunther. The fat man looked as if he were going to get up but sat back as we stepped in front of him.

"What's in the box?" I asked.

"Who are you?" asked the fat man.

I glanced at the soldier and the girl; they smiled at us, got up, and moved away hand in hand.

"We are two guys with guns," I said opening my jacket to show the .38 in my holster. Gunther opened his suit jacket.

The fat guy was sweating.

"I don't know. I'm supposed to give it to someone," he said.

"Who?" I asked.

"A girl or a guy. Girl's name's Blanche."

"And the guy's name?"

"Toby," he said.

Gunther looked up at me.

"I'm Toby," I said.

"And I'm Charlie Chaplin," said the fat man. "You're two robbers."

He started to get up. I opened my jacket and reached for the .38, hoping no one but he would see it. He sat again. I pulled out my wallet and flipped it open to my California Private Investigator's card. The fat guy squinted at it.

"Here," he said, handing me the box.

"Who gave it to you?" I asked.

He started to get up again. This time he made it. He was a lot bigger standing than I thought he'd be.

"I'm getting out of here," he said.

Gunther stood in his way. The fat man reached over and grabbed Gunther by the neck. I started to reach for the man's arm, but, before I could grab it, the man groaned and rose a foot in the air.

Behind him Jeremy had managed a bear hug. The man let go of Gunther who dropped to his feet rubbing his throat. The fat man's face was turning red. People were gathering to watch. Things like this happened in Pershing Square.

"He's having a heart attack," I told the crowd. "Give us room. I'm a doctor."

Jeremy let the fat man down. I moved close and said, "Who gave you the box?"

"Just a guy, here about an hour ago. Gave me the box, ten bucks, and told me what to do. I swear."

"What did this guy look like?"

"I don't know. Regular. About as big as you. Younger than you, I think. Almost skinny. Just a guy."

"Let him go, Jeremy," I said.

Jeremy released him.

"He'll be fine," I told the crowd. "False alarm. Just had a bunch of jujubes stuck in his throat.

The three of us moved down the path with our package. When we got to the street, I told Jeremy and Gunther to look around and see if anyone was watching us. Then I opened the package.

There was nothing in it but a note and a locket, a locket with two silver birds in flight. Fiona Sullivan's locket.

I read the note:

"Blanche, if you have received this, keep the locket but please call a Mr. Toby Peters whose phone number appears on the back of this note. Mr. Peters, if you are the recipient, you may keep this locket kindly given to me by Miss Sullivan. Inform your client that I am by no means finished with him."

There was no signature. I looked at the box. It told me nothing. I pocketed the note and locket and stood for a few seconds before it hit me.

"Chaplin," I said.

We ran out of the park in search of a phone and found a booth. I pulled out coins while Gunther and Jeremy stood in the open door.

There was no answer at the Chaplin number. I let it keep ringing. Then Chaplin's voice came on.

"It's Peters," I said. "Did Woodman get there?"

"The old gentleman with the large gun," he said. "Yes."

"There's a chance Sawyer may be back to see you," I said. "There's a good chance," I went on, touching the locket in my pocket, "he's murdered Fiona Sullivan."

"I see," Chaplin said. "And what is it you wish me to do?"

"I don't think it's a good idea to stay where you are until we find him."

"Perhaps you're right," he said with a deep sigh. "It certainly isn't safe here."

"Why?" I asked. "What happened?"

"Your Mr. Woodman almost accomplished what our Mr. Sawyer has been unable or unwilling to do. He came very close to killing me."

"Killing you?"

"Yes. My houseboy was about to clean one of the downstairs windows. He was on the outside. I was on the inside, trying to help him open the window. My houseboy, whose name is Ernest Wang, had a scraper in his hand. Apparently your Mr. Woodman thought he was an intruder bent on my destruction. He fired a shot, which shattered the window, thus making its cleaning no longer necessary. The shot came within a foot or so of hitting me. The bullet continued across the room and destroyed an expensive lamp."

"Is he there?"

"Woodman?" asked Chaplin, still very calm. "Here he is."

Woodman's voice was apologetic.

"Toby, it looked like a Jap with a gun was trying to break in. Listen, we all make mistakes."

I remembered that Woodman had made several mistakes

in the past that had left a trail of dead and wounded felons. I wondered how many of them might have been carrying cleaning implements that looked like guns.

"We all make mistakes," I agreed. Woodman had been one of them. "Fearaven with you?"

"No, couldn't make it. I'm on my own."

"Everything's taken care of now," I said. "You can go back home. I'll send you a check for the day."

"Hell," he said. "Okay. But listen. People make mistakes."

"I know," I said. "Let me talk to Chaplin."

Someone hit a horn driving past us as Chaplin returned to the phone.

"Sorry," I said.

"A window, a valuable lamp, a frightened houseboy, and an actor now considering the frailty of human existence," he said. "All with a single tiny projectile. One learns life's lessons in unexpected ways."

"One does," I said. "Will you move out again?"

"I will not," he said. "Welles is coming by in an hour to discuss *Lady Killer*. Then I have a meeting with a potential backer of the film upon which I am working. Besides, I do not share your belief that I may be in danger from our elusive Mr. Sawyer."

"Why?"

"I'm not quite sure yet. Intuition, perhaps. I want to discuss the entire scenario with Welles. I shall continue to calm my houseboy, have someone call a glazier, lament the passing of my lamp, and get back to work. It may be time, I fear, to call in the police."

"Maybe," I said.

"I've withstood so much negative publicity that this situation might well be only a dip in the road, dangerous but transitory. Now, if you will excuse me."

He hung up and so did I. I looked at Gunther and Jeremy and tried to come up with a plan.

"Perhaps we, Jeremy and I, should keep watch on Blanche Wiltsey," Gunther suggested.

"Good idea," I said.

"I suggest we approach her directly and give her some idea of our concern without providing information on the potential gravity of the situation," said Jeremy.

Sounded like the only way to handle it. There was no chance that the massive ex-wrestler and the tiny ex-circus performer could hide in a crowd.

"I'll try to find out what happened to Shelly," I said.

We had come to the Square in two cars, me and Gunther in my Crosley, Jeremy and Shelly in Shelly's 1938 Chevy. Jeremy and Gunther decided to take a cab to Coulter's. I headed back into the Square in search of Shelly and the cop. I couldn't find them. Shelly's car was still where he had parked it.

I went back to the phone booth and called my brother. He wasn't in but the desk sergeant, Marty Francesco, who picked up the call, recognized my voice.

"Toby," he said. "A lunatic was just brought in here. Says he knows you."

"Chubby guy with thick glasses?" I asked.

"The very one," Francesco said.

"Who has him?"

"He's going up for a talk with John C."

John C. was John Cawelti, a detective sergeant with something deeper than dislike for me.

"Why's he interested in a misdemeanor in the Square?"

"Heard the guy using your name. John C. got very interested."

"I'm on the way," I said.

"Sounds like that might be a good idea."

I hoped Phil was back at the Wilshire Station. When I got there, Francesco was at the downstairs desk hunched over and talking to an old man who seemed to be whispering.

Francesco was a patient man who looked like everyone's favorite uncle or the favorite uncle everyone would like to have. He was round, around fifty, with a permanent understanding smile on his face.

He motioned me over to him.

"And so," I heard the old man saying, "I can maybe buy one of those portable wire recorders, you know. Record what they say, bring it in. You find someone who understands Japanese and we catch 'em."

"Sounds like a good plan to me, Mr. Plano. A very good plan. Maybe you can pick up a recorder on the cheap side at a pawnshop. Don't let those spies catch you recording 'em though."

"I'll be careful," the old man said.

"And if they don't come back," Francesco said. "You can always record music or your favorite radio shows."

The old man nodded and shook the desk sergeant's hand. He turned, looked at me with suspicion, and went away satisfied.

"Phil's not back," Francesco said. "Cawelti's got your chubby guy in interrogation on two."

"Thanks, Marty," I said. "I won't tell Cawelti how I knew about this."

Francesco smiled and said, "Toby, I don't care if you tell

him. He can curse and scream and threaten and give me looks that would make Boris Karloff back away and it wouldn't get him anything but a tolerant smile from me. Hell, I'd welcome the diversion."

"*Ayuda me*," a woman behind me said, her voice quivering.

"*En que le puedo servir*," said Marty.

I got out of the way and headed up the wooden stairs.

The interrogation room was up the stairs, to the right, and past the squad room. It was purposely chosen for questioning suspects because it was at the end of the corridor behind a thick wooden door, away from where pleas, cries, shouting, and groans could be heard unless they were machine-gun loud, which they sometimes were.

My brother had a fondness for the room. It was probably John Cawelti's favorite place in the world: small, single bulb, no windows, wooden table with two chairs, and a phone book on the table. The phone book was used on the heads of suspects.

I didn't bother to knock. I opened the door and walked in. Cawelti was standing with both hands on the table. Shelly was on the other side of the table seated and sweating, his eyes and mouth open wide.

Cawelti's sleeves were rolled up. He was having a good time. He hadn't changed much in the years I had known him. He was about my height and weight but that was the end of the resemblance. John Cawelti had bright red hair parted straight down the middle. His face was pockmarked and angry and he always wore suspenders.

"Get out," he said, looking at me and standing back from the table.

"What are you holding him for?" I said calmly.

"You get a law degree or something?" Cawelti said, taking a step toward me.

"You want Marty Leib down here," I said. "I'll give him a call."

Marty Leib was, when I needed and could afford him, my lawyer. Marty knew everyone, everyone worth knowing. He could smear a cop with two phone calls. Cawelti knew it. He'd been smeared by Marty before.

"This man is a pervert," Cawelti said. "He was caught in Pershing Square with his pants down. When an officer questioned him, a couple of the pervert's friends tried to stop the officer. Description he gave was a guy who looked like an ex-pug and a dwarf. Sound like anybody we know?"

I didn't answer.

"Then this pervert assaulted the officer."

"I'm not a pervert," Shelly whined. "Tell him I'm a dentist."

"He's a dentist," I said.

"One count of public nudity and one count of assault on a police officer," Cawelti said. "Make a nice story in tomorrow's papers."

Shelly groaned.

"He wasn't nude," I said. "Call in the arresting cop."

"I wasn't nude," Shelly said.

"Report says he was nude," said Cawelti.

"I'd like to take a look at the report and talk to the arresting officer."

Cawelti laughed.

"Okay," I said. "Then maybe Phil will want to take a look at it and talk to the cop."

"I'm a respectable dentist," Shelly said. "Just look at me."

Cawelti and I didn't look at him. Our eyes were locked on each other's.

"You'll be running to big brother till he retires, which I hear might be soon."

I didn't say anything.

"Maybe no nudity. Maybe I misread the report," Cawelti said with a shrug.

"And maybe Dr. Minck, a respected member of his profession, lost his glasses and accidentally bumped into the arresting officer."

"That's right," Shelly bleated. "Lost my glasses. Blind as a cat, I mean a bat, without them. Accident. I'm always losing them, bumping into things, wandering into the street. Anyone can tell you."

"What do you want, John?" I asked.

"Read some notes," he said. "Some crap about five murders. Your name was mentioned. And our sweaty pervert here mentioned Charlie Chaplin's name."

"In passing," said Shelly. "Just in passing."

"Six murders, Charlie Chaplin," Cawelti said, shaking his head. "I'd like to know more. I'd like to know a lot more."

"Ask Phil," I said.

"I don't think so. I'm asking you."

"You let Dr. Minck go, and if and when I find the killer, I give you the collar."

He thought it over.

"And you forget he mentioned Charlie Chaplin," I added. "Providing."

"Providing," I agreed. "You get evidence and the collar."

"You're cheap goods, Peters, but your word is good. You can have butterball."

"I can go?" asked Shelly.

Cawelti nodded.

Shelly got up and hurried behind me to the door.

"Your word," Cawelti reminded me.

"And yours," I said.

He nodded.

I thought I knew why he hated me. We had too much in common. He lived alone in a one-room apartment. No family. He didn't drink though people thought he did, because of his pink face and because he hadn't saved any money. Even if I handed him Sawyer and Chaplin, he would never be anything more than he was. And I would never be more than I was. The difference was that I didn't fight my fate and Cawelti hated his. I wondered if he had anyone he could call a friend. I considered asking him but changed my mind.

"This is just between us," he said as I moved to the door.

That meant I wasn't to go to Phil. I didn't intend to. Phil might ask questions I didn't want to answer. Cawelti wanted the headline, the credit for catching the killer of six or more women.

"Between us," I agreed. "I hope this doesn't mean we're becoming friends."

"The first chance I get, I'll ram a nightstick up your . . ."

"One can't have too many enemies in our business," I stopped him.

"Get the fuck out of here," he said through his teeth.

I got out.

Shelly wasn't in the corridor. I found him outside the station waiting for me.

"Did you hear, see . . . false arrest," he sputtered. "He . . . I'm a dentist."

"Shel, you are a goddamn hero."

"He hit me with that phone bo. . . . That's right. I saved you in the Square. You and Gunther."

I hoped this meant that he would quickly forget his guilt about losing Fiona Sullivan. I decided not to tell Shelly about her locket in my pocket.

"You didn't get him," he said.

"No, we didn't," I said. "But thanks to you we're getting closer. I'll drive you back to your car."

"What time . . . ? I've got Mr. Kurtiser due in my office in twenty minutes for a file-down and four fillings."

"Let's not keep Mr. Kurtiser from his fate," I said, wondering where I was going to find Howard Sawyer and if I could do it before he dropped a rock on my head or Chaplin's.

Alice Pallis Butler was standing in the Farraday hall near the elevator on the sixth floor. Her arms were folded across her chest, and she looked as if she were ready for business. I hoped the business wasn't with me. I smiled, said, "How are you Alice?" and headed for the stairs.

Alice stepped in front of me. She was almost as big as Jeremy and nearly as strong. She had a pleasant, round face and short dark hair. Alice had a good smile. She wasn't wearing it now.

"Let's talk," she said.

"I . . . let's talk," I said. "Where?"

"Here is fine," she said.

She was wearing a blue cotton dress with an etched pink flower over her ample left breast. Her wide belt matched the flower.

"Jeremy," I said.

"We've had this talk before," she said.

"I know."

"But this one is different."

I waited. I could see that she was trying to figure out a way to tell me something that wasn't easy for her.

"I'll stop coming to him for help," I said.

"Because you're afraid of me?" she asked.

"No," I said. "Because I understand how you feel. The baby."

"Natasha? Yes," she said, glancing down the six-floor drop to the lobby below. "But the problem is Jeremy likes helping you. It makes him feel . . . I don't know, wanted. He's at peace with himself. Don't get me wrong. But there's a part of him that . . . I'm not doing this very well."

"You're doing fine, Alice," I said.

"He likes you," she said. "I can't keep saying 'no' to him. He's sensitive, Toby. He's a poet. But he's not a young man."

"He's a very strong old man," I said.

"Very strong in body. Very sensitive in soul. I didn't talk like that before I met Jeremy. I've told Jeremy everything I was before he met me. I don't think you want to hear it."

"Not unless you feel you have to tell me," I said.

"Only that I spent some time in prison," she said so softly that I almost missed it. "Not long, but enough. I'm not going to try to keep Jeremy locked in anything. I love him and he loves me and the baby. So, just take care of him while he's taking care of you."

"I will," I said. "I promise."

She touched my shoulder and smiled. Her touch was amazingly light. The touch told me there was no threat behind what she had just said. Then she turned and walked down the stairs ahead of me.

I listened to her footsteps go down two flights and turn

down the corridor moving toward her office/apartment. When the door closed with an echo, I started down.

On the street I went to the corner and stepped into Manny's. There were no customers. Just Manny behind the counter with a cup of coffee and his newspaper. Manny had been looking gaunt with the strain of worrying about all of his relatives fighting the Nazis and the Japanese.

He read every word of the newspaper every day and knew what was going on all over the world. He looked up at me with resigned eyes and said, "Burma."

"Burma," I repeated, sitting at the counter. Manny poured me a cup of coffee. I added some sugar and waited for more about Burma, not wanting to think about Alice walking down those stairs in front of me, walking to a real home and family.

"We pounded the Japs from the air in Burma while the Brits were fighting on the ground, but it's not over. The Japs have more than eighty thousand men in Burma. It's gonna take everything: planes, men, sea power. It's not gonna be over for a long time. The Japs aren't gonna give up easy. Our boys, lots of them, are gonna be in for it."

I knew he meant his own boys, his own family.

"Yeah," I said in a flash of brilliance.

"I'm goin' home," he said, taking off his apron. "Finish up. I'm closing."

I knew what he meant. He wanted to be with his wife Rosie and his sister and brother-in-law who lived with them. He wanted to be with family.

I gulped down the coffee and told Manny I'd see him tomorrow.

"Right," he said. "Coffee's on me."

CHAPTER
10

I SHOULDN'T HAVE done it. I knew it then. I know it now, but there are loose ends that demand to be tied. They sit there in the back of our minds, reminding us when we least expect it that they won't go away. There were places I should have been, things I could have been doing.

For example, I could have taken on the job of watching Chaplin as soon as I left the Wilshire Station. I could have gone over the clippings Gunther had found in Sawyer's drawer. I could have gone back to Blanche Wiltsey to try to find out what connection she might have to Sawyer. I could have consulted with Juanita though I knew she would just give me more questions and no understandable answers.

Instead, I went to the travel office my ex-wife Ann owned and managed. She had started working for an airline when she left me and kept moving up her ladder while I sat on the lowest rung of mine. Since she had married Preston Stewart, the couple had made the newspapers from time to time with her described as a successful woman in business and him described as the dashing Preston Stewart.

The office was on corner of Sepulveda and Mitchell, a renovated storefront building with a tasteful sign in both of the downstairs windows that proclaimed in flowing black script that the would-be traveler was about to enter the offices of Ann Stewart Travel. Before Ann moved in, the top floor had been leased to a bookie named Cyril Petrano under the name of Smith Enterprises. The bottom storefront floor had been The Culver City Bar. The windows had been painted black when it was a bar. They were now clear and always clean so visitors and passersby could see busy men and women on the phones, hurrying with papers in their hands, talking to customers seated by their desks.

"Can I help you?" asked the receptionist, a thin girl with severe dark hair, large teeth and smile, and a well-pressed dark suit.

You can help me catch a murderer, I thought. You can tell me you're a specialist in whatever was going to kill my sister-in-law, Ruth. You can try to convince me that I am right up there with Gary Cooper or Robert Taylor or Preston Stewart.

"Ann Stewart," I said.

"She's with a client," the girl said brightly. "Can someone else help you?"

Anita Maloney was the most likely substitute, but Anita was behind a drugstore counter serving BLTs on white toast at Mack's Pharmacy.

"No," I said, looking at my dad's watch on my wrist. It told me that I didn't know what time it was. "It's important. Can you tell her Toby is here?"

"I don't think I can disturb her," the girl said sweetly. "Mrs. Millbanks can . . ."

"No," I said. "Mrs. Millbanks can't. Just tell her Toby is here."

"Toby who?"

"The Toby who used to be her husband," I said.

"Oh," said the girl. "Oh."

She picked up the phone and dialed a single number.

Ann Stewart Travel looked like an office movie set with the agents and customers as busy extras. Voices were low. There was no loud laughter.

"I'm sorry," the girl said softly into the phone, "but there is a gentleman here who says his name is Toby and that he wants to see you." The girl nodded while Ann talked and then looked up at me. "What did you want to see her about?"

"Matters of love, life, and death," I said. "Urgent matters."

"He says 'urgent matters of life and death,'" the girl said and then listened before saying, "Yes."

She hung up and looked at me.

"At the rear of the office, up the stairs, first door on the left."

"Thank you," I said.

"I think I just messed up," the girl said.

"How?"

"This is my first day on the job. I was told not to disturb her." She bit her lower lip. "Oh well, if she fires me, I can go back to being a carhop at Howie's Drive-In in the Valley. Tips are good but the guys . . ."

"She won't fire you," I said with a grin.

The grin didn't seem to reassure her.

"I don't make as much money here," she said, "but I get to sit all day instead of standing most of the night."

"And wearing those little costumes," I said with sympathy.

"You know how many times a night you get your bottom pinched or touched at a drive-in?"

"Me? None."

"I meant me. Six, seven times, and other stuff. I'm a high school graduate."

"Louise," came the voice of a man at a nearby desk.

"Yes sir," said the former and maybe soon-to-be-again carhop.

He had a sagging face with sad eyes and a head of black hair shining with Wildroot. He didn't have to say more.

"I'm sorry," she said.

The guy with the sagging face shook his head at the quality of help one could get nowadays. I winked at Louise the receptionist and moved toward the back of the office and to the stairway. Ann's office was just where Louise had said it would be. Her name was on it in small, tasteful, black block letters. I knocked.

The door opened and I let a fidgety little man clutching a briefcase to his chest pass by me and head for the stairs. Ann stood about four feet away. I could smell her. It was more than faint perfume.

Her dark suit with a white blouse wasn't much different from that of Louise the receptionist, but Ann, who was now forty-six, filled it with authority and a full figure.

"Life and death," she said.

She looked great, dark hair piled on her head without a loose strand, smooth pale skin, full red lips that matched her fingernails, and a barely tolerant look on her face.

"You look great," I said.

"Thank you. And you look pretty much the same as always."

159

"I know a compliment when I hear one," I said. "And I don't think I just heard one."

"Life and death," she repeated.

I reached back to close the door. She stepped past me and pulled it wide open.

"How are you?"

"Fine." Her hands arms were folded impatiently across her chest. "Life and death, Toby, remember?"

"Ruth is dying," I said.

"I'm sorry," she said, letting her arms drop to her side. "Is she home?" I nodded. "I'll call her."

"She'll like that. She always liked you."

"And I like her," Ann said. "Toby, you didn't come here to tell me about Ruth. You could have done that on the phone."

"I wanted to see you. That's the 'life' part."

She shook her head and looked at the ceiling before looking back at me. She was saying 'not again' without having to use the words.

"Toby, please . . ."

"You've asked me for help more than once since you left me," I reminded her. "Now I'm asking you for help. You owe me a few minutes, Ann."

"All right," she said, moving behind her desk and sitting down. "You have a few minutes. And don't close that door."

"You're doing well," I said, looking around the office. "Leather sofa, big desk, nice paintings on the wall."

She looked at her watch.

"Impulse," I said.

"What is?"

"Coming here."

"That's it?" she said with a sigh.

160

I shrugged.

"Wanted to see you, hear your voice. I didn't feel like doing anything but shake your hand and wish you good luck."

"You did that at the wedding, remember? And?"

"Let's have lunch, talk. You know." I said.

"I don't think so. Are you still seeing Anita . . . ?"

"Maloney," I said. "Yeah."

"I like her. I wanted a husband. Maybe she'll be satisfied with an irresponsible playmate. Don't lose her."

I didn't know what to say.

She stood up again, came around the desk, stepped in front of me, and kissed me. Her smell was the good past remembered. She stepped back.

"Preston and I are having a party next month. His new movie." she said. "I'll send you and Anita an invitation. And I'll call Ruth."

In other words, she would behave, as always, like a responsible adult. I felt as if my mother, who I never knew, had handed me my school lunch in a brown bag and told me to have a nice day and remember my spelling words.

"What's the movie? Preston's new movie?"

"*Dark Streets*," she said. "He plays a private detective. If it does well, they're thinking of turning it into a series."

The unkindest cut of all.

I left. She closed the door behind me.

I stood in front of her door and reached into my pocket. I pulled out Fiona Sullivan's two-bird locket and held it in the palm of my hand. I had long ago lost the woman on the other side of the door. I had a feeling I had also lost the woman whose locket I was looking at. I went back down the stairs.

"How did it go?" Louise the receptionist asked, glancing back at the saggy-faced man who was on the phone.

"It could have been better," I said.

"She's not going to fire me?"

"No," said. Ann wasn't the firing kind.

"Good," Louise said. "Thanks."

I nodded and went back out onto Sepulveda. I had gotten my periodic dose of Ann. It made me feel worse, but I needed it. As soon as I could, I'd take Anita to the movies. We'd have a burger or maybe even a steak and we'd go back to her apartment and talk. And that would be good.

My Crosley was wedged in between two big cars. At least they seemed big to me. All cars were big compared to the Crosley. It took me six twists and turns in the space before I could escape without touching the bumper of the car in front of me.

No one seemed to be following me. Sawyer was only one man and he had too many possible targets: me, Chaplin, Blanche Wiltsey, and who knows how many others.

I headed for Fiona Sullivan's house. I didn't expect to find her there listening to Schubert and jumping out of her chair to thank me for returning her locket. I don't know what I expected or hoped for.

The street was quiet. The sky was clear. The thick trees around the house kept it in shade. I parked and went to the door. It was locked. I knocked, waited, gave up, and went around to the back of the house. The kitchen door was locked. I peered through a window, saw nothing, and tried to push the window open. It was locked, but the lock was a loose hook held in by a screw. Trees behind the house gave me cover. I pushed the window hard, loosened the screw, pushed again, and felt the window groan open. I climbed in and closed the window behind me.

The phone was ringing. I had a fair idea of the layout of

the house and a clear memory of where the phone was. I walked through the afternoon gray shadows to the living room. The phone kept ringing. I picked it up.

"Peters," came the voice I had heard on the phone at the home of the deceased Elsie Pultman. He had followed me.

"Yes," I said.

"You got my gift?"

"I got it," I said, touching the locket in my pocket.

"Would you do me a favor and give it to Blanche for me? Fiona won't be needing it anymore."

"We'll see," I said.

"You won't find anything there," he said. "I took everything I needed."

"Thanks."

"Thought I'd save you some time," he said. "I've changed my mind about you. I'm feeling euphoric. I have a deal for you and Chaplin. He doesn't make his movie about me and I don't pay a visit to the lovely little Blanche."

"That's up to Chaplin," I said.

"I'll tell you what," he went on. "I throw in a promise. I won't kill any more women. I'll stop. Just like that. No more. I'll disappear."

"That's not up to me."

"Sure it is," he said.

"The police know all about you now," I said. "And I made a deal with a cop to turn you in."

"I wish you hadn't," he said. "But still, to show my good faith, I promise you I will not harm Blanche Wiltsey. You can believe me."

"Why not? You haven't lied to me in the past."

"Maybe we're becoming something like friends," he said, pleased with himself.

"I'm not smart," I said. "But I'm stubborn. I don't give up. I'm going to find you."

"How?" he asked.

That I didn't know.

"I have to go. Chaplin drops the project, I disappear. That's the deal on the table. There is no other. There's no room for negotiation."

"One question," I said. "Since you're so goddamn smart, what difference does it make if Chaplin makes his movie? You're going to disappear. No one is ever going to find you, remember?"

"You miss the point," he said. "I'm writing a book about my adventures. When I'm old I plan to find an agent who'll get it published and a producer who'll make a movie. It's a very interesting story."

"Then you'll be caught," I said.

"Then I'll be old already and famous. My mother never believed I'd amount to anything. My father shared her opinion. They are both gone except in my memory. Their deaths will be in my book. I dispatched them elegantly and with flair. Good-bye."

He hung up. I had no reason to take his word about anything he had told me. He was definitely nearby. My .38 was still in the holster under my jacket. If I stayed here too long, he'd know I didn't take his word that he had cleaned everything out. Actually, I believed him, but I didn't want him to know I did.

I sat in the most comfortable chair in the room with my gun in my hand and waited. I'm not very good at waiting, and I didn't know how much time was passing. I found an old issue of *Life* with the Sphinx on the cover and read about how they were sandbagging the neck to protect it from German bombers and tanks. I seemed to remember reading it before. I couldn't figure out why the Nazis would want to blow off the head of the Sphinx, but there were a lot of things I didn't understand about the Nazis.

When I finished the article, I went back to the kitchen and climbed out the way I had come in, pulling the window down behind me.

Sawyer had said he wasn't going to kill Blanche Wiltsey. I believed him on that one too, but I wasn't ready to take his word. I walked around the building and into two cops in uniforms carrying guns in their hands. I stopped.

"Hands in the air, slow and easy," said one cop, who was about my age, a little on the thin side in a uniform that sagged. He looked as if he had lost some weight recently. The other cop was bigger, a little younger, and wore a snug uniform and a squint.

I put my hands up. The thin cop stepped forward, reached under my jacket, and took my .38 out of my holster.

"I'm a private investigator," I said. "I've got my card with me. I've got a permit for that weapon."

"You have a permit to break into a crime scene?" he asked.

"I didn't break in anywhere," I said.

"We got a call from a neighbor saying someone fitting your description had just climbed into this house through a back window."

"You said this was a crime scene?" I asked.

"Blood all over the bathroom?" said the dull-looking cop with the squint. "No body."

"Felix," said the thin cop in a distinctly warning tone.

"I'm a friend of the woman who lives here," I said.

"Neighbor suggested we might want to search you," said

the thin cop, stepping in front of me carefully and starting to go through my pockets.

He came up with a stick of Beeman's Pepsin Chewing Gum, my car keys, some change, and Fiona Sullivan's locket. He held the locket up.

"Yours?" he asked. "Or did you pick it up inside?"

"It's a gift for my girlfriend," I said.

"Looks old," he said. "Looks silver."

"I got it at a pawnshop," I said.

"Let's go tell it to a detective," the thin guy said, handing me my change, gum, and keys, and keeping the locket.

"You know Phil Pevsner out of the Wilshire?" I asked, my hands still in the air.

"Yeah," said the thin cop.

"My brother," I said.

"Then," said the cop, "let's all three of us go over and see him."

And that's what we did. The thin cop rode with me in the Crosley with a gun in his hand. The squinter drove in a patrol car behind us.

They delivered me to Phil's office door. Before the thin cop could knock, a loud sound of something inside shook the door. We heard a groan. No one in the squad room paid any attention. Such noises were common in my brother's office.

The cop knocked.

"Come in," my brother called.

We went in. Phil had his jacket off and his sleeves rolled up. The jacket was draped over his desk. Sagging against the wall was John Cawelti, shaking his head slowly back and forth.

"What now?" Phil asked, looking at me, his fists doubled.

He wasn't finished with whatever he had been discussing with Cawelti.

"Found this guy in the house of an assumed murder victim," said the thin cop, ignoring the redheaded detective trying to clear his head. "Says he's your brother."

"He's my brother," Phil said. "Whose house?"

"A Miss Fiona Sullivan," said the thin cop.

Phil looked at Cawelti and said, "We'll finish talking later."

Cawelti tried to regain some minimal dignity but his wobbly legs weren't cooperating. He gave me a less than pleasant smile as he staggered past us and into the squad room.

"I wasn't in the house," I said. "They picked me up outside the house."

Phil was looking at his fists.

"He had this on him," said the thin cop, holding out the locket and my gun.

Phil looked up without any great interest and took the locket and gun.

"I think he took the bird thing from the house," said the thin cop. "Says he got it from a pawnshop."

"Leave him here," said Phil. "I'll take care of it."

"I think my partner and I should . . ." the thin cop began, but Phil cut him off with a shout.

"Get the hell out of here."

The two uniformed cops got the hell out of the office, closing the door behind them. Phil was looking at the locket now, playing with it.

"You went to her house," he said, moving around to sit at his desk.

"Yes," I said.

"You find anything?"

"No."

"You found this."

I told him the story of the box in the Square, about Fiona Sullivan having worn the locket when I had last seen her, about the call from Sawyer, about Jeremy and Gunther watching Blanche Wiltsey. I threw in my meeting with Cawelti.

"He just told me about that," Phil said, playing with the locket. "I don't give a crap about who gets credit for catching this lunatic. I want him caught. You can tell Butler and Wherthman to go home. I'll put a couple of men on the Wiltsey kid. Toby, there's still something you're holding back."

"What? I told you about Chaplin."

"Something else."

"I need a couple of days," I said.

"Fine, two days," he said, looking at the locket. "Two days."

"Two days," I agreed.

He put the locket in his top desk drawer, handed me my gun, folded his hands on his desk, and looked over at me.

"Now it's your turn to get the hell out of here," he said.

I got out, feeling better about my brother. The last time I had seen him he had been a mellow impersonator I didn't recognize. In the last few minutes I'd seen the almost total return of the Phil Pevsner I recognized. This was a dangerous Phil Pevsner. This was my brother.

When I got back to my office, Violet told me that, the night before, Al Reasoner had died after a TKO in the tenth round by Freddie Dawson. That, and Shelly's singing beyond the reception room door, did nothing to brighten my day.

"And Mr. Butler called," she said. "He'll call back. Said to tell you if I saw you that everything was quiet."

"Thanks," I said and went through the door in time to witness Shelly, bloody pliers clamping a tooth held high, singing out the words to "Mississippi Mud" in triumph.

The woman in the chair, her mouth and eyes wide open in terror, looked up at her tooth. Shelly noticed me through his thick lenses, removed the cigar from his mouth, and said, "Toby, sometimes life is very good."

"Sometimes it is," I agreed and ducked into my office, trying to ignore the plea in the eyes of Shelly's reclined victim.

The window in my office was closed. I moved behind my desk and opened it to a hint of fresh air tinged with the smell of Chinese food and the view of a small open lot behind the Farraday where a rusted and wheel-less old Pontiac sagged on a sea of cracked concrete.

The phone rang. It was Jeremy. He told me Blanche Wiltsey was home. I told him the police were taking over and that he and Gunther were relieved with my thanks.

"Did you find Dr. Minck?" he asked.

"He's alive, well, free, and in his office doing his best in his never-ending assault on mankind."

We hung up. I ignored the six envelopes that had come in the mail and placed neatly on my desk by Violet. None of the letters was personal. They were all attempts to get at money I didn't have enough of.

I was reaching for the phone, not sure of who I was going to call, when the door to my office opened. A short man with yellow hair showing under his fedora and a pair of round, horn-rimmed glasses on his nose stepped in and plunged his hands into the pockets of his trench coat.

"Recognize me?" he asked in an accent that sounded like Texas.

He started to pull something out of his pocket. There was no place to hide, no place to go, except out the window, and not enough time for me to get my .38 out of my holster.

Charlie Chaplin removed his empty hand from his pocket, took off his hat, wig, and glasses, and unbuttoned his coat.

"Uncomfortably warm," he said in his own voice as he sat and looked at the walls of my office. "Charming painting," he said.

"It's a Dalí," I said.

Chaplin turned to me.

"Really."

"I did some work for him," I explained.

"An odd little man," Chaplin said smoothing his hair with his hands. "I admire his showmanship."

I looked at him. He raised his eyebrows and looked back at me.

"You're wondering about the disguise," he said. "People seldom recognize me on the street, but I wanted to do something that might deceive even someone who knew me."

"I was deceived," I said.

"Good. Very good." He rubbed his hands together. "I believe I have an idea about our Mr. Sawyer."

Since I didn't have any of my own, I sat and waited.

"I may well be wrong," he went on. "However, it is relatively easy to put to the test. Elsie Pultman is being buried today."

"Buried," I repeated.

"Read it in the obituary notice of the newspaper," he said. "And?"

"You and I shall attend the graveside service," he said. "I in disguise, you arriving after me a few minutes later and standing some distance from me showing no sign of knowing me."

"You think Sawyer will show up for the burial?" I asked.

"If my theory is correct, he shall be there."

"Why? You think he showed up at the funerals of all those other women? Likes to see them buried?"

"Not quite," said Chaplin with a distinct twinkle. "Not quite."

"What time is the burial?" I asked.

"Just before sundown," he said. "We have a bit of time, but not much. I came by taxi. I assume your car is serviceable."

"It's serviceable," I said.

"Good, then I have one more question."

"Shoot," I said.

Chaplin turned his head to the door and asked, "What is that bizarre man doing to that woman?"

"That's Sheldon Minck. He's the dentist from the train."

"Yes, but . . ."

"It's better not to think about it," I advised. "When we go out, don't talk to him. I'll tell him later that you're a mobster."

"Someone should rescue the woman in the chair," he said, rising.

"There'll just be another to take her place in an hour. The world is filled with people who miss all the warning signs, and wind up under his lamp and dull instruments."

Chaplin held up his hands to indicate that he would surrender to the inevitable. I put my jacket back on, and we went out the door.

171

CHAPTER
11

TRAFFIC WAS HEAVY. We had a lot of time to talk, and, since Chaplin was in a good mood, he did most of the talking. That was fine with me.

"I have made mistakes," he said, looking out the window. "I have also made people laugh and cry. I have made a great deal of money and I have, I must admit, been less than delicate in my dealings with women. I take it you are not married?"

"Not anymore," I said.

"Ah," he said with a sigh. "I can't seem to resist the institution, but I'm confident that Oona, who is no impulsive mistake, will be my final foray into matrimony. Are you on good terms with your former wife?"

"Hard to say."

"I try to retain a cordial but distant friendship with ex-spouses," he said. "I think Paulette and I will remain on good terms. I hear she's going to marry Burgess Meredith. Distant, cordial relationship, Toby."

"I'll try it," I said.

We reached the cemetery just before the sun went down. Chaplin put on his disguise and got out of the car in front of the cemetery gate. Down the road beyond the open gate we could see about four cars parked along a gravel path.

"Give me five minutes," he said. "Then drive in and walk slowly to the gravesite."

"How do you know this is the right funeral?" I asked.

"I called. There ain't but one at this hour," Chaplin said in his Texas accent. "*Hasta la vista.*"

He opened the door, got out, and headed for the parked cars. I watched him walk away in a deliberate stride unlike his normal, faster gait.

I was supposed to follow him in five minutes. I couldn't be sure about the five minutes so I turned on the radio and listened to a little of Quincy Howe and the news. Roosevelt was hopping around the world and an announcer told me to buy 666 Cold Tablets. I figured that took five minutes. I drove up the gravel path toward the gravesite, the setting sun to my left. I parked behind a big Chrysler four-door, got out, and walked toward the group of people around an open grave.

The casket of Elsie Pultman rested on a stand near the hole. A man wearing a black suit and black hat with a Bible tucked under his arm was speaking in a solemn tone.

". . . and what else can we say about this woman? Elsie Pultman was not known as a generous woman, not known as a devout or kind woman, not known as a friendly woman, but she hurt no one, donated frugally to the Red Cross, and spoke well of President Roosevelt. She also saved large amounts of grease in tin cans to support the war effort.

Her family and friends have come to bid her farewell and we ask that our Lord take her into his realm with love and understanding."

I looked around the small gathering. Chaplin stood next to two old women on one side of the grave. On the other, just behind the casket were the two men in work clothes who would be lowering the casket into the grave. A large mound of dirt stood behind them with two shovels next to the pile. A few feet from them stood a tall woman in black with a wide hat and a handkerchief to her eyes. She was a good-looking woman of about forty with large earrings and a wide red mouth. Next to her stood a man about her age with a dark mustache and hair brushed back. He wore a well-pressed suit and a sad look on his downcast face.

I approached slowly. Eyes turned in my direction. I could see Chaplin the Texan looking at the man with the Bible, the grieving man and woman, the old ladies, and even the two grave diggers. I stopped about ten feet from them all.

"You may lower the casket," the man with the Bible said.

The two workmen did just that, with ropes and expertise. When the casket was in place, the man with the Bible nodded at the man with the mustache who reached down, picked up some dirt, and dropped it on the casket. I could hear the dirt hit the wood. Then the good-looking woman in black did the same thing and stood back.

"Ashes to ashes. Dust to dust," the man with the Bible said and stood back.

The old women moved over to shake the hand of the man who had conducted the service and then they moved to the fellow with the mustache, who, it seemed, was being comforted by the tall woman at his side.

I stepped closer as Chaplin went around the headstone and moved to the mourning man.

The sun was almost down now but I could read the engraving on the big gray headstone:

"Elsie Frances Pultman, 1869–1943, In Loving Memory, Jeffrey."

I didn't move forward. Chaplin then moved off to talk to the man who had delivered the eulogy. The conversation was brief.

I stood watching while the procession moved away leaving the workmen to fill in the grave. When the mourners were almost at their cars, Chaplin moved to my side.

"I was right," he said.

"About what?"

"You didn't recognize them?" he asked.

"Who?"

"Ah, perhaps it's my years in show business. Makeup and disguise are essences of our craft. The tall, rather handsome woman was Fiona Sullivan," he said.

"Fiona Sul . . ."

"Remember, she was a makeup artist," he said. "My guess is that we just witnessed the usual appearance of Fiona Sullivan. The dowdy spinster look she presented to us was the disguise."

I suddenly remembered Mrs. Plaut telling me that Fiona Sullivan was considered to be a good-looking woman given to too much makeup.

The cars were pulling away.

"I don't get it," I said.

"And there is more not to get," Chaplin said as we moved slowly toward my car and the sun fell further. "The man with the mustache was Howard Sawyer, or at least he has used the name Howard Sawyer."

"Who is he?"

"The nephew of Elsie Pultman, Jeffrey," said Chaplin. "Jeffrey Pultman, her only heir. The late Miss Pultman, I have discovered, was a very wealthy woman."

"So, he killed his aunt for the money," I said. "Why did he kill the others?"

"I don't think he did," said Chaplin, removing his disguise. "I think he wanted us to think he did. Let's go over it."

The cars were gone now. Only Chaplin and I were left in the growing darkness.

"He comes to my door, orders me to stop working on my project about a man who goes around killing women. He plants the idea that he has been doing just that. He also mentions that I should stay away from Fiona Sullivan. I had no idea who Fiona Sullivan might be. He wanted me to find Fiona Sullivan."

I was beginning to get it.

"So you hire me. I find Fiona Sullivan. She says Howard Sawyer has a room in her house. She sees to it that Gunther finds the hidden clippings that give us a list of dead women."

"Suggesting," Chaplin said, "that they are former victims of the mad Howard Sawyer."

"But," I said, "they're not. They're just clippings he cut about dead women."

"Precisely, and then when Fiona Sullivan disappeared . . ."

"We figured she was another victim. And Blanche Wiltsey was just a name he plucked from a phone book."

"Thus, we, and then the police, believed that Sawyer had

not only murdered again, but that Blanche Wiltsey is to be his next victim."

"Fiona Sullivan's locket," I said. "He got it to me to make us think she was dead."

"There has been but one person murdered by Jeffrey Pultman playing the fictitious Howard Sawyer, and that victim was his aunt."

We were in the Crosley now.

"Now they're getting away," I said.

"No," said Chaplin. "Seeing you may make our Mr. Pultman very nervous, but he may also reason that you are just following up, doing your job. He has no reason, or none with any certainty, to think that you are aware of who he is. Besides, after going through this elaborate charade, I doubt if he will run off without his inheritance."

I drove down the gravel path.

"So where is he?" I asked.

"Staying in his late aunt's house in Venice," said Chaplin. "The Reverend was kind enough to tell me where I might, as an old friend of Mrs. Pultman, pay a condolence call."

"It's time to turn this over to the police," I said.

"Turn what over?" Chaplin asked. "I walk into the police station." He mimed opening a door. "Sit in front of a detective." He pretended to sit, defying gravity. "I smile." He gave a comic toothy grin. "And then I tell him my story. Does he leap up and say 'Let's go grab the vile murderer?' No, he says, 'Come back when you've got something besides your theory about what happened.'"

Chaplin stood straight.

"So?" I asked.

"So I suggest we pay a condolence call on the grieving

nephew. We come up with a plan by which he will provide us with a confession or evidence."

"Or he decides to kill us."

"Unlikely," said Chaplin. "And you are armed."

"You're enjoying this, aren't you?" I asked.

"Immensely," Chaplin said with a deep breath. "Shall we go?"

On the way to Venice, Chaplin was in a good mood.

"Let's play one of my favorite games," he said. "Let us cast our little adventure as if it were going to be a movie."

Traffic wasn't too bad. Rush hour was over. That meant traffic wasn't great, but it didn't make you want to get out and walk. I didn't feel like playing any more games.

"I, of course," said Chaplin, "would play myself."

"How about Spencer Tracy playing me?"

"I would think more in terms of Nat Pendleton. For Dr. Minck, I would say Lou Costello. Mr. Wherthman gives us little choice but Billy Barty. Mrs. Plaut would need Marjorie Main. And Jeremy Butler. Ah, we would need Mike Mazurki."

"And Jeffrey Pultman?"

"A tour-de-force bit of casting," he said. "Buster Keaton. It would rekindle his career."

I didn't like any of it, but I kept driving.

"May I?" asked Chaplin reaching for the radio.

"Help yourself."

He turned the dial until he found something classical featuring a piano. He knew the music and hummed along. When we were a few blocks from Elsie Pultman's house, I pulled into a parking spot.

"Why are we stopping?" Chaplin asked.

"So he doesn't see us drive up."

"But we want him to see us," said Chaplin.

"Not if he has a gun."

"Which he will not use," countered Chaplin with a slight air of impatience. "He doesn't want to risk losing his aunt's money. He'll bluff. We'll pretend."

"It's dangerous," I said, pulling out of the space and continuing down the street.

"I think not, but I relish the idea of walking up to his door and surprising him as he surprised me earlier this week. Perhaps I should douse myself with water and carry a cane?"

"Perhaps we should do some more thinking," I said, finding a space directly across the street from the Pultman house.

"I have experience with people pretending to be what they are not," he said.

"And I have experience with people who shoot at me."

"Then," said Chaplin getting out of the car, "we shall combine our experience and catch a killer."

I got out and followed him across the street. He stepped up to the door and knocked.

"Maybe he's not here," I said. "I don't see any of the cars from the cemetery."

"He may have a garage," Chaplin said.

He knocked again.

"Someone looked through that window over us," I said, putting my right hand near my belt where I could pluck out my gun.

Chaplin continued to knock. He tried the door. Something creaked inside the house. Footsteps moved down the stairs and then away from the door.

"Back door," Chaplin whispered.

We ran around the house, ducking low so whoever was

inside might not see us if they glanced out a window. It turned out to be a tie.

Fiona Sullivan was stepping out the door as we rounded the corner.

"Miss Sullivan," Chaplin said.

She turned, tall, startled. Mrs. Plaut had said she was a good-looking woman. Mrs. Plaut had been right.

"Yes," she said, trying to keep calm, her hand on the doorknob, ready to duck back in.

"Shall we talk?" asked Chaplin.

"About what?" she asked as if she had no idea of who we were.

"Good," said Chaplin. "I see how this scene will have to be played. Do you contend that you do not know who we are?"

"Who are you?" she asked.

"I am Charles Chaplin and this is Toby Peters. You and I met briefly on a train."

"I don't recall," she said.

It was my turn to get into the game. I pulled out my gun and aimed it at her.

"No more," I said, pretending that I had lost my patience and possibly my reason. "I'm not going to play the sap for you or anyone else."

That was more or less the line I remembered Bogart saying to Mary Astor in *The Maltese Falcon*.

"Now, now," Chaplin said soothingly, putting an hand on my arm. "I'm sure Miss Sullivan will cooperate."

"I'm tired of talking," I ranted. "I'm tired of being run around the park like a windup monkey. I'm giving her five seconds to turn Pultman over or I'm going to shoot her god-damn knees off."

"What is he talking about?" she asked with a touch of real alarm.

I was getting through to her so I went on. I waved off Chaplin's hand and he staggered back. I thought he was overdoing it a little, but we'd criticize each other's performance later.

"He suffered a head wound in the war," Chaplin said. "When he gets confused . . . I hear that he ran over a blind man on Hollywood Boulevard who reminded him of Erwin Rommel."

"Well," she said, "stop him."

"No use," said Chaplin with a deep sigh. "He'll just shoot me too."

"I'll shoot anybody," I said. "I want answers. I want the world to make sense again. I don't want boxes with lockets. I don't want bodies parked in front of my house. Mr. Keen gets answers. The Durango Kid gets answers. The goddamn Shadow gets answers. I don't get answers, then I get bodies. Lady, say your prayers."

Chaplin's back was to Fiona Sullivan now. He was rolling his eyes to let me know that I was going too far, but for the first time I understood how an actor must feel when he's improvising. I didn't want applause. I wanted the audience, Fiona Sullivan, to believe.

"I've done nothing illegal," she said, looking at Chaplin for help.

"You aided a murderer," Chaplin answered.

"I didn't know," she pleaded. "Believe me."

Neither of us believed her, but Chaplin said, "I believe you. He told you it was an elaborate hoax, that he was . . . ?"

She struggled for an answer while I made growling sounds and shifted from foot to foot, refingering the gun in my hand.

"He was trying to frighten his aunt," she said. "She had a weak heart."

"He wanted to frighten her to death?" asked Chaplin.

"Yes," she said.

Her story stunk. I took a step forward. She put her back against the door.

"Where is he?" I said between clenched teeth.

"Calm yourself, Mr. Peters," Chaplin said. "The lady is cooperating. She had no idea Jeffrey Pultman planned to murder his aunt."

"No idea at all," she said, putting one hand to her mouth. "When I found out he killed her, I wanted to get out, but I was afraid of him."

"And now you are prepared to tell the police everything this monster did?" asked Chaplin.

"Yes," she cried, looking at me.

"She's lying," I cried. "Let me kill her. My head hurts."

"Take one of your pills, quickly," Chaplin said, reaching into his pocket and pulling out a small purple bottle with a prescription label. He opened the bottle, poured a round gray tablet into his palm and opened his mouth to demonstrate what I should do. I opened my mouth wide. He popped the tablet onto my tongue and I gulped it down. What the hell had he given me?

"Miss Sullivan," Chaplin said. "I have no doubt the police will hold you in no way responsible. You have been a poor victim forced to cooperate to save your life. No jury would convict you."

Right, I thought, no jury of chimpanzees.

"Where is he?" I said, reaching up to touch my head.

"You'd best tell us," Chaplin said.

"He went to the lawyer's office to finalize papers," she said, looking at my gun waving from side to side.

"And who might his lawyer be?" asked Chaplin.

"Alexander Fuller of Leib, Johnston, and Fuller in Culver City."

Marty Leib was my lawyer. I had never met Fuller or Johnston. The phone was ringing inside the house. Fiona Sullivan pushed open the door and disappeared. We ran after her. By the time we got through the kitchen, she was on the phone in the front hall weeping.

"Jeffrey," she cried. "They're here. They're going to kill me if I don't . . ."

I grabbed the phone from her. She backed up with a scream. Chaplin took the phone from me and said, "Pultman, I'm afraid the performance is over."

I kept the gun aimed at Fiona Sullivan, who slumped back against the wall, her mascara and makeup running because of her tears. Chaplin held the phone away from his ear so I could listen.

"You were the old man at the cemetery," he said calmly.

"I was," Chaplin admitted.

"Is Peters there with you?"

"He is," said Chaplin. "I'm afraid you've killed your aunt for nothing."

"No," he said. "For everything. I've got the papers. I'm at the bank now waiting for a cashier's check from the president. I've sold everything for half of what it's worth, which means I'm walking out of here with three hundred thousand dollars."

"You weren't planning to come back here for Miss Sullivan," he said, looking at Fiona who was wiping her face with her sleeve. She now looked a bit more like the woman I had seen in her home and on the train.

Chaplin shook his head to show her what Pultman's answer had been.

"No," she said. "No."

"I'm a man of many names and faces," Jeffrey Pultman said happily. "In a few hours, I'll be wearing one of them and moving somewhere where I can enjoy good food, the company of lovely women, and the delicious pleasure of the show I've staged."

"Jeffrey," Fiona shouted, pushing away from the wall and trying to get her hands on the phone. She didn't seem to care about the mad Toby Peters with the gun anymore.

I held her back. She clawed at my face. Chaplin went on calmly, "Well, I've learned through bitter experience that one must accept defeat with good grace and applaud a fine performance."

"Thank you," I heard Pultman say. "Coming from you that's a compliment I'll remember. I am, as you have guessed, an actor."

I shoved Fiona away, having a serious instant in which I actually considered shooting her in the foot.

"And a fine one too. May I suggest Mexico?" Chaplin said. Pultman laughed.

"You may suggest," he said, "but I'm keeping my destination to myself. You understand."

"I do indeed," said Chaplin.

"The president is coming back now. He's holding what looks like a check in both hands. Good luck with *Lady Killer*."

Pultman hung up. Fiona got past me and grabbed the phone.

"*Jeffrey*," she shouted. "Jeffrey."

"He's gone," Chaplin said with a deep sigh. "I'm afraid the police will have no one but you to hang."

"No," she said, dropping the phone. "Jeffrey wouldn't . . ."

"He just did," I said, resuming my normal tone.

"If you help us," Chaplin said. "If we can catch Pultman and you testify against him, I think you can be reasonably certain of a very light sentence."

"Or none at all," I threw in.

"Quite possibly," Chaplin agreed. "Can we get you a drink?"

She nodded "yes," and Chaplin led her into the living room where he went to a liquor cabinet we had seen when we had been here before. He opened it and said, "Port, sherry, a Dewars?"

"Dewars," she said. "No. Make that port. I've never tasted port."

"I like that," said Chaplin, pulling a notebook out of his jacket pocket and writing something. He looked at what he had written and read it, "I've never tasted port." Then he turned to me and said, "That would be a perfect line for a man who was being offered a last drink before his execution." Then he put the notebook back in his pocket.

"Did he have a passport?" I asked Fiona, who was seated while we stood over her.

She took a sip of the wine and nodded "yes."

"He mentioned good food," Chaplin said. "What kind of food is he most fond of?"

"Food? Steak, fine steaks," she said.

"Does he speak any foreign languages?" Chaplin asked.

She took another sip and coughed before she answered.

"A little Spanish and something else."

"What?" I asked.

"I'm trying to think. I never heard him speak it. Something his parents spoke. What difference does it make?"

Chaplin rested an elbow in the palm of one hand and tapped at his lower lip.

"I've got an idea," I said, moving into the hall and picking up the phone. I could see Chaplin and Fiona Sullivan in the living room looking at me.

I dialed Marty Leib's office. I knew the number well. A secretary answered and I told her who I was and that it was a matter of life and death. She put me through and I heard Marty's deep, even voice.

"Yes."

"Marty, Alexander Fuller had a client in there a little while ago, a Jeffrey Pultman."

"Is that a question?"

"No, but I'm coming to one. Fuller handled his aunt's estate."

"Yes," he said.

"And your firm approved transfer of everything to Jeffrey Pultman in one session?"

"No," he said. "As I understand it, Pultman asked Fuller about setting up the transfer some time ago."

"While his aunt was alive?"

"Toby, what is this about?"

"Pultman killed his aunt," I said.

There was no sound but Marty's breathing on the other end of the phone.

"I'll have to check with Alex, but as I recall, Pultman said weeks ago that she was dying," Marty answered. "He had medical papers substantiating her illness. According to Alex

Fuller, Pultman was an impatient man, an impatient man offering to pay a substantial fee for very quick service upon the aunt's demise."

"What bank?"

"First Federal, I think," Marty said.

"Did he give Fuller any hint of where he was going, what he was going to do?"

"You want me to ask him?"

"Yes."

"Now?"

"Right now."

The pause was long.

"Hang on. I'll see if he's free."

"Interrupt him," I said.

Marty didn't answer. I heard the phone clunk on his mahogany desk. I looked at Chaplin and Fiona again. They were both trying to figure out what was going on. Chaplin seemed to get it. Fiona didn't. Marty came back on the phone in about three minutes.

"Pultman said nothing about where he was going," said Marty. "And he got everything but what she was buried in: the dress, her mother's necklace and ring."

"One more question. You have all of Elsie Pultman's papers. Birth certificate, all that stuff."

"We have. Alex handed her file to me."

"Where was she born?"

Chaplin smiled. He could see where I was going.

"Let me take a look." There was a pause while the chair creaked from Marty's rising. He was a big man who moved very slowly.

I waited. Chaplin watched. Fiona sipped.

"San Francisco," Marty said.

"She had a sister or brother. Jeffrey's parents."

"Brother."

"Where were her parents from? You have that?"

"Yes, Portugal. And, before you ask, though I don't know where this is going, the brother was older than Elsie. He was born in Portugal as was his wife, Jeffrey's mother."

"Portugal," I repeated.

"Sunny Portugal," Marty repeated slowly. "Any other questions? I'm in no hurry."

"No," I said. "That'll do it."

"I'll send the bill to your office," he said.

"Bill?"

"For this consultation," he said. "One hour. Thirty-two dollars."

He hung up.

"Portuguese?" I said, looking at Fiona.

"I think so," she said.

Chaplin was smiling.

"He can't get to Portugal," he said.

"At least not till the war is over," I picked up.

"Therefore," Chaplin said, and we both answered:

"Brazil."

CHAPTER
12

I CALLED THE Los Angeles airport. There were no direct flights to Brazil. There were, however, two ways to get there by plane. One was a flight to Mexico City with a connection to Caracas and on to Rio. Another was to New Orleans, then to Havana, and any of five ways from Havana to Brazil. I didn't bother to check with any of the airlines to find out if a Jeffrey Pultman or a Howard Sawyer was booked on that first step to Brazil. He wouldn't be using his own name, and he would almost certainly be in some kind of disguise.

"Now what?" asked Chaplin.

Fiona sat weeping. I thought, took a deep breath, and dialed a number I wasn't supposed to have. Six rings and an answer.

"Yes," came a woman's voice.

"I'd like to talk to Mrs. Stewart," I said.

"May I say who's calling?"

"Toby Peters. Tell her it's life and death."

The woman put down the phone. Minutes were racing by.

"Peters?" came Preston Stewart's familiar voice.

"Hello, Preston," I said.

"Ann told me about your visit earlier this afternoon," he said calmly.

"This is about business," I said.

"Peters, please leave her alone," he said with real concern. "She's been through . . . well, you know most of what she's been through. She's a tough woman, but your harassment doesn't make her life any easier."

"Stewart," I said. "I need her help and I need it fast. You can listen in on an extension."

"Thanks, but I don't think I need your permission."

"I didn't . . . please. It is really a matter of life and death this time."

Silence. Preston Stewart was thinking. I remembered his pose in *Shadow of a Gun* when he had to decide how he was going to answer the question of a Gestapo colonel.

"All right," he said. "I'll tell her, but I don't know if she'll talk to you."

More silence. Then I could hear Stewart and Ann talking. I couldn't make out what they were saying. Then Ann came on the phone.

"Life and death," she said, sounding very tired.

"Ann, if you wanted to get to Brazil, how would you do it with the least likelihood of anyone asking questions about who you were?"

"You're serious?"

"Dead serious," I said. "A man murdered an old woman. I think he's trying to get to Brazil, fast."

Ann knew more about travel than anyone I could think of.

She was an expert and I knew her mind would grab a question like this and go into professional mode.

"I wouldn't go by boat," she said. "Too dangerous. Not many boats are taking passengers because of the German submarines. You could fly out of Los Angeles to . . ."

"That I've checked," I said.

"But if you didn't want to be spotted at the airport," she went on, "and if you had a passport, the best thing to do would be to drive to Mexico and catch a flight from there."

That was it. Pultman might figure that it was possible we would be checking the airports. He would probably play it safe, drive north to Canada or east to anywhere.

"Thanks, Ann," I said.

"Don't call me anymore, Toby," she said. "Please."

"Okay."

"I've got a headache, and Preston and I need some rest. Whatever you're doing, be careful, but don't call me."

"I'll be . . . ," I said, but before I could say "careful" she had hung up.

Chaplin was looking at me for some sign.

"I think he's heading by car to the Mexican border," I said.

"And then on to Brazil," Chaplin supplied, nodding his head in understanding. "You think this, but you are not certain?"

"No, but it makes sense."

"Then let's go with your judgment," he said. "Your next call will have to be to the police."

It was my turn to nod.

"And it is now essential that I completely reveal my part in this affair," he said.

"I can't see a way around it. Fiona talks. You talk. We try to convince the police to check cars at the border."

"But," asked Chaplin reasonably, "if Pultman has a false passport and has altered his appearance . . . ? Ah, I see. You propose that I fly to the Mexican border ahead of him and check every man, woman, and tall child going across."

"You know what he looks like. You'd recognize him through a disguise," I said.

"I am confident that I would," Chaplin agreed with a humble bow of his head.

"Then . . . ," I began.

"Let us go," he finished.

I called my brother's office. He was still there. I told him what was going on, that Fiona Sullivan was ready to talk, that Pultman was getting away, possibly with murder. Phil did not like that and he didn't like the game Pultman had played with the deaths of the other women.

"Where are you?" he asked.

I told him.

"I'll make some calls, have a car pick Chaplin up," he said. "I'm going to put my job on the line, Tobias," he said. "I'm going to get a plane for Chaplin. You bring the Sullivan woman here, now. Can you handle her alone?"

"Yes," I said.

"Then get started."

He hung up. I told Chaplin the plan. He approved.

"There is always the chance he'll slip through," Chaplin said.

"Tell the border guards who you are," I said. "Get their names and addresses and tell them you'll send them autographed photographs."

"Considering the current attitude toward me, they may not be so inclined," he said.

"They're human," I answered. "They like telling stories

about celebrities they've met. Even the cops and prison guards wanted Capone's autograph."

"Not a flattering comparison," said Chaplin.

"Sorry," I said. "I've got to get Fiona into the city. Good luck."

Two hours later, Fiona Sullivan, having already given her statement and still declaring her innocence, had been taken away. I sat in my brother's office. We drank coffee. A little after eight he called home, talked to Ruth and the boys, and said he would be there as soon as he could.

He held out the phone.

"Nathan wants to talk to you."

I took the phone.

"Hi Nate," I said.

"Uncle Toby," he came back soberly. "David says you never shot anybody."

It was Nate's favorite subject. I looked at Phil, sleeves rolled up, definitely in need of a shave. The gray stubble on his face and the distant look in his eyes reminded me of how old we both were.

"I've told you," I said.

"No, I mean really. I'm old enough."

"I shot one man when I was a police officer and one since I've been a private investigator. Neither of them died. I also shot myself once."

"I remember," Nate said. "My dad won't tell us how many people he shot."

"I know," I said, looking at Phil whose eyes were on me, warning. "You'll have to talk to him about that."

"He won't talk about it," Nate said with disappointment.

"Say hello to your mom and Dave for me," I said. "Get some sleep."

"First we listen to Baby Snooks," he said. "I think we're old enough for *Inner Sanctum* too."

"That's up to your mom and dad," I said.

"Yeah," Nate answered and then hung up.

At 8:15, Phil called down and got a uniformed cop to pick up some sandwiches. He didn't want to leave the phone.

An hour later Cawelti came into the room, his face red.

"What's going on?" he said to me.

"Get out of here," Phil said, rubbing his eyes.

"This piece of crap brother of yours said he'd give me the lady killer," Cawelti said, standing his ground, posturing but ready to retreat if Phil decided to charge. "Now I hear he's giving it to you. I had a deal with you, Peters. I let that fat little pervert go."

"You can have the collar," Phil said. "Now get out of here."

Cawelti turned to Phil, who was still rubbing his eyes.

"What?"

"You can have it," Phil said. "But it's not going to get you headlines or medals. He only killed one woman."

"Bullshit," said Cawelti.

"It's the truth," I said.

"Now, for the last time," Phil said, opening his eyes wide to ward off weariness. "Get out."

"Don't jerk me around," Cawelti said. "I've got a right to be here."

Phil shook his head and started to get up.

"John," I said. "If I were you, I'd start running."

Cawelti looked at my brother. He saw a rhino ready to charge. He made it to the door and through it as Phil took two quick strides toward him. Then Phil turned to me.

"Don't say it," he said.

"I wasn't going to say anything."

"Don't even think it then," he said, fist clenched.

I knew that look. I had felt those fists. He wanted something or someone to hit.

"Cawelti is a decent enough cop," he said. "And he's never going to get anywhere. No one likes him. If he has a mother, I don't think she even likes him. I don't think he likes himself. He is one sad, lonely, and angry man. That doesn't mean I wouldn't have thrown him through the wall."

I didn't say anything.

We waited. Around eleven, a call came through. Phil listened, said "Okay" four times, and hung up. It was an army sergeant at the Mexican border. He said Chaplin was checking everyone out and, so far, no Pultman.

"He's not going through," Phil said. "Not tonight. And Chaplin needs some sleep. Hell, maybe he's in Pittsburgh or Havana by now. Maybe he's not done here. Maybe there's something more he can pluck from his dead aunt's hand."

That rang a bell. There was something else. The question was, what was it worth and how big a chance was Pultman willing to take?

"I guess I'll head home," I said. "You should too."

"Right," he said. "Ruth'll wait up for me."

He slipped on his jacket and we walked out together. When we got outside, I headed for my car and he headed in the opposite direction for his Ford in the parking lot.

I drove to the nearest phone booth, pulled out all my change and my notebook, and dialed a number. Four rings.

"Yes?"

"Marty?"

"Who is this?"

"Toby," I said.

"What did they arrest you for?" he asked, no sign of having been awakened from sleep.

"Nothing," I said. "I have a question."

"Which couldn't wait till the morning," he said.

"Which couldn't wait till the morning, and I know it will cost me thirty-two dollars."

"Sixty," said Marty Leib. "Night rates. Ask your question."

"You said Elsie Pultman was buried wearing a necklace and a ring, her mother's."

"That is what I said."

"Did Fuller's notes say what they were worth?"

"Yes, but it was only an estimate based on an appraisal, not market sale price."

"How much?"

"The necklace, as I recall, was worth about twenty thousand, the ring fifteen or sixteen thousand. A waste to bury them, but legal. We've made a note in our files. In a few years we'll return to the issue and see if some sympathetic judge will be willing to consider reviewing Miss Pultman's decision."

"Thanks," I said.

"Legal advice and representation are what I'm here for," he said evenly.

I hung up and headed for the cemetery. If Jeffrey Pultman was going after his aunt's jewels, he would wait till after midnight to be sure no one would see him. There was probably an all-night caretaker. If I was right about all this, the caretaker was in deep trouble.

The iron gates of the cemetery were closed and locked. Inside the gates, about thirty yards away I could see the small stone building. Lights were on inside. I considered rattling the gate but Pultman, if he was there, might hear me.

I started climbing. It was fine until I got to the black iron points at the top. The gate was attached to the high wall around the cemetery. I pulled myself up to the wall and sat looking toward the graves.

A small light was visible about a hundred yards away.

I couldn't see anything but the light and the silhouettes of headstones. I didn't hear anything that sounded like digging.

I climbed down into the cemetery, managing to grab my flashlight just as it was about to fall from my pocket. Then I headed for the stone office building.

The windows were clear. I looked in and saw nothing.

I went to the front of the small building. The door was open. Just an office, some chairs, filing cabinets, a desk, and a map of the cemetery on one wall.

I remembered the place where Elsie Pultman had been buried well enough to get back to it. There was a phone. All I needed was something to back up my intuition. I found it sitting in the closet I opened.

The old man was seated inside the closet in a chair. He was tied tight with rope and a cloth around his mouth.

His eyes opened wide when I opened the door. He was having trouble breathing. I took the cloth from his mouth. He sputtered and gasped for air.

"You all right?" I asked.

"Hell no," he said.

He was thin, pale faced, with scraggly white hair. He wore a pair of dark pants and an old blue shirt in addition to a look of confusion.

"Grave robbers," he said as I cut him free with my pocketknife. "That's my bet."

"He hurt you?"

"No," said the old man. "Just my feelings. Been here going on eighteen years. This is the first time anything like this has happened. Oh, we get some kids climbing in sometimes but . . . hell, what are we talking for? Call the police."

"You do that," I said. "I'm going to see who the guy is who did this to you. He's about my height, a little lighter, about forty, right?"

"Happened fast and I lost my glasses," the old man said, steadying himself with one hand on the chair and starting to get up.

I found his glasses on the floor and handed them to him. He put them on and looked at me.

"Who are you?" he asked.

"Private investigator. The guy who did this to you is a killer."

"I'm calling the police," he said, moving to the phone.

I went out the door and into the night. I didn't know how long it would take the police to get here or even which police might come. I figured the fastest I could get real help would be fifteen minutes unless I got lucky with a patrol car.

The light I was following was weak but I didn't want to turn on my flashlight. Then I heard the sound. Shovel digging in, dirt falling on the ground.

I rounded a tree, gun in hand, and found myself looking at Jeffrey Pultman, at least the head and arms of Jeffrey Pultman. He was deep in his aunt's grave and shoveling dirt onto a pile a few feet away. I moved closer. He didn't see me, didn't look up. He grunted and dug. When I was about a dozen feet away, he let out a satisfied sound as his shovel hit the casket.

I stood waiting while he backed up, straddled the sides of the hole he had dug, and opened the casket. I kept watching while he leaned over and came up with the necklace and ring. The light from his flashlight next to the grave hit him from behind. He was a black outline right out of a Karloff movie.

Then I turned on my flashlight, pointed the beam at him, and held up my gun.

"Greed," I said. "Gets 'em every time."

He looked at me, jewels in one hand, the other hand at his side. I stepped forward.

"Don't reach for anything," I said. "Just stand there."

His face and clothes were spotted with dirt. He didn't look surprised or even worried. He smiled. He was no longer the bespectacled blond of the afternoon. His hair was dark and straight; a strand stuck to his forehead.

"You didn't figure this out," he said. "You're not smart enough."

"Maybe you're not as smart as you think you are," I said. "You make everything too complicated. Best way to get away with a crime is to just do it and walk away."

"No fun in that," said Pultman calmly. "I'm an actor. I wrote a script for myself and lived it. The money will feel so much better when I'm able to look back at my performance."

"Greed," I said again.

"Right," he agreed. "I admit it. I couldn't resist these. But Peters, all this performance lacked was applause."

He held up the jewels.

I took another cautious step forward.

"And now?" he asked.

"We stand here and wait for the police," I said.

"Can't do that," he said. "It's not the end I planned. In my tale, the bad guy, that's me, gets away. Well, actually I'm not a bad guy, just an impatient, clever adventurer."

"Whatever you say. Just stand there."

"Can't do that," he repeated, dropping into the grave, and ducking down so I couldn't see him.

"That's fine with me," I said. "You stay down there and I stay up here. We can tell each other stories while we wait."

But Pultman had a different plan. He stood up suddenly, shovel in hand, and heaved it in my direction. I ducked to the right, fired, and missed as he came at me out of the hole. I slipped and backed away. I'd lost my flashlight but I could see his outline. I fired again. I think I came close. But I didn't hit him. He picked up the shovel and took a swing in my direction. I fell backward to the ground and scrambled away losing my gun.

He took another swing with the shovel and caught my ankle. The pain was lightning. He stood over me now, shovel raised high.

Instead of backing up, I lunged forward, my head ramming into his stomach. He staggered back and I looked around for my gun. My flashlight was on the ground facing the grave. No gun, but I did see the necklace and ring. I crawled forward a few feet and grabbed them. Pultman was getting up now. He hadn't lost his grip on the shovel. I got to my feet and ran. My ankle hurt like hell, but I ran expecting a sharp steel edge cutting into my skull. Then I heard the shot.

Instead of coming after me, Pultman had gone for my gun and found it. He didn't seem to be any better a shot than I was, but let's be fair: It was dark, I was running, and he was trying to catch his breath.

I headed away, toward a far wall. The flashlight beam hit about fifteen feet to my left. I tripped and went down on my knees, facing the headstone of Samuel Sidney Talevest. I struggled behind Sam's headstone just before the beam of the flashlight hit it and moved on.

And this is where I started telling you my story.

"Peters," Pultman called out as the rain came. "Throw

out the jewels. I'll take them and go. I don't want to leave a trail of bodies behind me."

I kept my mouth shut and stuffed the jewels in my pocket.

"Be reasonable," he said with a laugh as the rain began to fall. "This is nothing for you to die over."

I could hear his footsteps under the rain. My best guess from his voice and the sound of his feet was that he was to my left and behind me. I took a chance, turned in pain, and peeked around the headstone.

I could see the flashlight's beam going slowly, lighting the back of a headstone. He moved to another. I didn't have much time. I got out from behind the headstone and crept as quietly as I could on my hands and knees back toward the grave of Elsie Pultman. With luck and the rain covering the sound I was making, I had a chance to get back there. I wasn't sure what I planned to do when I arrived. I doubted if I could crawl all the way to the gate without being caught.

Over my shoulder I could see Pultman moving forward, jabbing light behind tombstones including that of the late Sam Talevest.

"Peters, I'm withdrawing my offer. I'm wet. I'm impatient, and you may have been telling the truth when you said the police were on the way. And so, I'll give you this small victory and get out of here. I'll just have to rewrite the ending of the tale, a bittersweet victory for the elusive brilliant criminal."

I had crawled while he talked, crawled all the way to the open grave of Elsie Pultman. I flopped over the side and landed inside the open casket looking down at Elsie whose makeup, with the rain beating down on her face, was in urgent need of the talents of someone like Fiona Sullivan.

No sounds now but the rain. I knelt, careful not to step on Elsie. I'd give Jeffrey about four minutes to get away, then I'd get out of the grave and make my way back to the caretaker.

Suddenly the light hit my face and I looked up. I hoped it was the police, but I knew who it was even before I heard his voice.

"Surprise," he said. "I was always good at hide-and-seek when I was a kid."

He lowered the flashlight a little, though the beam was still in my face. Now I saw the wet figure Charlie Chaplin had opened his door to four nights earlier.

"Hand me the jewels," he said, holding out his hand.

I reached into my pocket, listening for sirens I didn't hear. I gave him the jewels.

"I rather like your dogged determination, Peters," he said. "But I'm afraid I'll have to shoot you and bury you with dear auntie. Will anyone miss you?"

I thought about that for an instant. Gunther, Jeremy, Anita, probably Shelly, my brother, Ruth, my nephews, maybe Mrs. Plaut for a day or two. The list was short.

"A few people," I said. "Time for a few questions?"

"You're stalling," he said.

"You're right," I agreed. "But I also have a few questions."

I was hoping the ego he strutted and the chance to perform a little while longer would give me a few minutes.

"Ask your questions, Scheherazade."

It was raining harder now, beating like a drum on the casket.

"Why didn't you wait until your aunt died?"

"Good question. She wrote me a letter asking if I would mind if half of her money went to a war orphans charity when she died. She was certain I wouldn't mind and reassured me that there would be plenty for me."

"But she was wrong."

"I called her and told her that leaving half her money to charity was a wonderful idea. I asked her to wait a few months till I got there so I could be a proud witness to her new will and together we could make out one for me in which I left everything to charity."

"Generous," I said.

"Thank you. I came to Los Angeles immediately, contacted Fiona Sullivan with whom I had worked years ago and who had more than a crush on me. My charm blossomed with my plan."

"You never planned to share with Fiona Sullivan," I said.

"Not for a moment. I considered eliminating her, but, as I said before, I didn't want to leave a trail of bodies behind me, at least not people I had really killed. Enough?"

"Never," I said.

"I think that will have to do it," he said, aiming the gun at my face. "I'm wet and, frankly, a bit tired, and I have a late plane to catch. So . . ."

My legs gave way, my ankle burning with agony. The shot was loud, echoing in the grave. I felt no pain. I was still alive. I waited for another shot. It came, but it didn't seem as close. I closed my eyes waiting for the third and final shot. He couldn't miss a third time. At this range with a trapped target, even I couldn't miss a third time. I remembered Juanita's premonition of me and a dead woman I shouldn't step on.

I looked up at the flashlight beam above me.

He stood with the gun hanging down at his side. He looked smaller and older than he had a few seconds ago.

"You all right?" asked the caretaker.

"No," I said, "but I'm alive."

"Best crawl out of there and close the box on the poor lady."

I groaned my way over the edge of the grave and lay on

my back with the rain beating against my face. Then I heard the sirens.

"Took a shot at him. Guess I scared him off," the caretaker said. "Tell you the truth, I tried to hit him, but my glasses are wet."

"I'll settle for scaring him off," I said. "Thanks. You're sure he's gone?"

"Watched him run for the gate," he said. "Considered taking another shot, but I wanted to see if you were alive first."

"I'm alive," I said.

He helped me up, and, with my arm on his shoulder, I hobbled toward the gate. The sirens were closer, much closer.

"Let's go into the office," the caretaker suggested.

"No, just let me out the gate and tell the police what happened."

"What did happen?"

"The late Miss Pultman's nephew dug her up and stole the jewels she was wearing," I said.

"And what do I tell them about you?" he asked as we reached the gate and he pulled out a thick ring of keys.

"What do you know about me?"

"Not a whole hell of a lot," he said, opening the gate.

"Then that's what you tell them."

"Why can't you stay and tell 'em yourself?"

"The nephew killed his aunt and he's going to get away if I stay here and get pulled in by the police. By the time they believe me, our boy will be halfway to who knows where."

He nodded and I hobbled through the gate and toward my car. It was a long hobble. He stood here watching and called, "Good luck."

I waved back over my shoulder and got into my Crosley and closed the door just as a cop car, siren going, pulled up in front of the cemetery. I slouched down, reached up, and tilted the mirror so I could see what was happening.

Two cops in raincoats got out reasonably fast and approached the caretaker. They started to talk. The caretaker didn't look my way. He turned, and the cops followed him toward the rows of buried dead.

I sat up and started the car. I drove with one foot. The ankle was bad enough without giving it a chore. Shifting gears and hitting the brake with the same foot wasn't easy.

Wet, in pain, and trying to think, I drove. Who could I call? Phil? It was after midnight. I would wake Ruth and I'd probably have a hard time making him believe that my latest hunch, even though it was supported by the words of Jeffrey Pultman, was right. I had already been wrong once tonight and he was going to have some tough questions to answer the next day about flying Chaplin to the Mexican border.

Gunther? The phone would ring in the hall. I'd eventually get him, but what could he do? He could give me advice, which I badly needed. But by the time we figured something out, Pultman would be gone. I rejected Jeremy for the same reason, and there was, anyway, a likelihood that his wife Alice would answer the phone and be less than happy with me. Shelly wasn't even a serious consideration. Chaplin? I'd already sent him to the Mexican border and back.

I was on my own and out of ideas. Then I realized there was someone nearby I could probably count on. I drove, windshield wipers scraping against glass, trying to think.

In about ten minutes, I pulled in front of a two-level court-yard of apartment buildings off of Third Street. I hobbled to the door to Anita Maloney's apartment and knocked.

"You're about nineteen hours early for our date," she said.

I didn't smile. Even though it was after midnight and she

was wearing a blue robe, it didn't look as if I had awakened her. She had a cup of something hot in her hand.

"You look awful," she said, holding the door open for me to hobble in. "What happened?"

"Long story," I said. "I've got to tell it fast and use your telephone. Your daughter here?"

Anita had a grown daughter who frequently spent the night if she was having husband trouble.

"No," she said.

"Have anything dry that might fit me?" I asked starting to sit in a chair in the small living room.

"Wait," she said. "You're wet. Sit in that one."

I moved to a wooden armless chair near the telephone table. She handed me the cup and I drank. It was tea.

"Thanks."

"Get out of those clothes," she said. "I think I have some things from my ex in a box. They'll come close."

I sat and drank the tea. Then I took off my clothes, all of them, after taking everything from my pockets and removing my empty holster. I dropped the pile on the floor.

Anita came back in with clothes in her arms. She looked at me.

"You should spend more time in the sun," she said, handing me the bundle.

"I'll make a note," I said.

"So," she said as I dressed. "What's going on?"

I told her fast. The clothes fit reasonably well: trousers, a tan shirt, dark sox. I did without underwear.

"And he thinks he killed you?" she asked.

"Not sure," I said. "But I think so. I was lucky. He was using my gun, which, along with its owner, has a long history of unreliability. Why aren't you in bed?"

"Did the shift till ten at Mack's," she said, sitting across from me. "Couldn't sleep. I was reading when you knocked. What now?"

I reached for the phone book and said, "I make some calls."

And I did. I called the Los Angeles Airport and was told by the woman who answered that there were no flights out after midnight. She also told me there were no scheduled flights out after midnight at any of the airports within a hundred miles. I thanked her and asked Anita for a pencil and some paper. She got them while I was looking through the book for private airports. I found six of them in greater Los Angeles and started dialing as Anita handed me pencil and paper.

The first three I got, in order, were a janitor, a mechanic, and a man who had just flown in on his private plane from San Diego. All three said there were no flights going out till morning. At number four I reached a man who said "Watkins Airport."

He was a pilot and he did have a charter going out in about an hour.

"Who's the charter?"

"Who are you?" he asked.

"Mikelewski of Air National Defense," I said. "We have reason to believe a Nazi collaborator is planning to fly out of the Los Angeles area in the next few hours."

"My charter's for a Mr. and Mrs. Walter Cannon."

"You've met Cannon?"

"Yep."

"Average height, a little on the thin side, about forty?"

"Nope, about six-one, over two hundred pounds, and not a day under sixty."

"Where are they going?"

"Denver," he said.

"Why so late?"

"Didn't say," the pilot said. "He's paying premium. I'm collecting premium. I didn't ask."

I tried the next airport. A telephone operator came on and said the number was no longer in service and the business, which had been there, was closed for the duration of the war.

That left one, the Richard Barth Airport in Glendale. The remarkably bright voice of a young woman answered, "Barth Airport."

"You're open," I said.

"Twenty-four hours," she said. "Family-owned business."

"You have a flight out in the next few hours?"

"Four of them," she said.

"Who are the passengers?"

She didn't ask me for identification, so I gave her none.

"No passengers," she said. "Freight only. Flights to Fresno, San Francisco, Santa Barbara, and Reno. Can't tell you the cargo without approval of the clients."

"No passengers?"

"Not a one. Not ever."

"Thanks," I said and hung up. I looked at Anita and shook my head.

"Well?"

"Watkins Airport in Burbank," I said. "Couple named Cannon are flying to Denver. That's about it."

"Maybe this Jeffrey Pultman lied about having to catch a flight?"

"He thinks he killed me," I said. "He told me because he was about to shoot me."

"But he didn't shoot you."

"I don't think he knows that."

"Slim lead, Toby," she said.

I got up. When my left leg touched the ground, I yelped and sat back. There was no chance I could put my own shoes back on.

"Sit there," Anita said, getting up.

She was gone for about two minutes. When she came back, she was wearing a green pullover dress. She handed me three aspirin and a glass of water, and knelt in front of me with a wide roll of white adhesive tape.

"Advantage of working in a drugstore," she said, starting to tape my ankle. "You get things free. This is going to hurt."

"It already does," I said. But what she did hurt even more.

"That's it," she said. "See if you can stand."

I stood. It wasn't good. It wasn't impossible.

"I can make it," I said.

She helped me put on my shoes and sox and I started for the door.

"I'm driving," she said.

"Anita, there's no . . ."

"It wasn't a question Toby," she said. "It was a statement of fact. You can't make it to Burbank on that ankle, not if you want to use the brakes. Let's go."

We went. She had a car but we took mine. Anita could drive. She liked to drive.

"You have to get up for work in the morning," I said.

"I've got an intimate confession, Toby," she said over the scrape of the windshield wipers. "I've got insomnia. Since I was in high school. I don't usually fall asleep till dawn. That's why I work the noon to seven shift."

"Bad dreams?" I asked.

"Bad memories," she said.

It took us forty minutes to get through Coldwater Canyon and across to Watkins Airport. The rain had stopped, but the streets were still wet. There was traffic, but not much. There's always some traffic in Los Angeles.

Watkins Airport was in the field outside of town on La Tuna Canyon Road. I knew the area. I had grown up in Glendale, not that far away. I had been a cop who sometimes found himself on unpaved roads at night.

We drove through the wide-open, steel-mesh gates and headed for the brightly lit little wooden building with a big painted sign that read "Watkins Airport." A single covered lamp illuminated the sign. There was a nightly blackout but the airport didn't seem to be in touch with the world and the war. A single car, a two-door, definitely prewar car was parked in front of the building.

Seven small planes stood silently, propellers toward us, next to a long narrow runway that ran deep into the darkness. Anita drove as close to the wooden building as she could get and we got out.

The pain was bearable. We went to the door and into the office. An overstuffed man in an unzipped flight jacket sat reading a copy of *Look* magazine. The man wore thick glasses and definitely needed dental work.

"I called you," I said. "Mikelewski."

"Air National Defense," he said. "Yeah."

"The Cannons."

"Not here yet," he said looking at his watch. "They said they'd be here before one, but I'm in no particular hurry. They paid in advance."

It was almost one.

"You don't think they're Nazis, do you?" he asked, putting his magazine aside.

"We'll see," I said. "Miss Rand and I will wait and see."

"Fine with me," he said. "I got paid even if you drag 'em away in chains. You armed?"

"No," I said.

"What if they are?" he asked.

"I'll worry about that when I determine if they're the ones we're looking for."

"Well," the big man said. "I'll worry about it right now if it's all the same to you."

He got up, crossed the room, opened a desk drawer, and came up with a large revolver that looked as if it could have been taken from the dead cold hands of Billy the Kid.

"We get vandals," he explained. "War going on. Airplane parts are worth beaucoup dollars."

"They're coming," said Anita, touching my arm.

The pilot and I paused and listened. A car was coming.

"What's your name?" I asked.

"Glen Overbee," he said.

"Put the gun in your belt and zip up," I said. "Just in case."

The car stopped in front of the door. The car door opened and closed. A few seconds later a man stepped in, big, around sixty, definitely not Pultman. He looked around at the three of us.

"We're ready," he said to Overbee. "My wife's in the car."

"Tell her to come on in," Overbee said, moving around the desk. "I'll get the plane ready."

"We'll wait outside," Cannon said, glancing nervously at us.

"My name's Mikelewski," I said. "This is Miss Rand. Air National Defense."

Cannon nodded and said to Overbee, "I'd like to get going."

Overbee nodded, pursed his lips, and moved to the door, pausing to look at me. I shook my head "no" to let him know this wasn't the man I was looking for.

"Do you mind telling us why you're taking a charter flight to Denver at one in the morning?" I asked.

"Business," he said, moving toward the door.

"What kind of business?" I asked.

"Government contract," he said. "Hush-hush. I'm not at liberty to talk about it. Some British and Canadian Air Force officers want it this way. Now, if you'll excuse me."

He was out the door before I could say more. Anita and I moved to the window. Overbee had turned some runway lights on. He was climbing up a wooden step stool through the plane's open door.

"Now what?" Anita asked.

"We watch," I said. And we did.

The plane's engine started and Overbee leaned out the door and waved at the car. Cannon got out, walked around the car, opened the door, and helped his wife out. She was about average height, dark hair, a bit too much makeup. She wore a thin brown coat with the collar up. She carried a medium-sized leather suitcase. He took her hand and they hurried toward the plane.

"Why isn't he carrying the suitcase?" Anita asked.

"Think about it," I said. "Then answer a question."

"You want to know if that's a woman?" Anita asked.

"That's what I want to know," I said.

"It isn't," she said. "Makeup job is good. But that's not a woman's run. Steps are too long. And look at the way she's carrying her arms."

We were out the door and into the night. Cannon and Pultman had a thirty-foot lead on us and I was hopping on a bad ankle. Overbee was leaning out of the plane watching. I held up my hand and pointed at the Cannons. He nodded. When the couple was within a few feet of the step stool, Overbee came out with his six-shooter aimed at them.

The sound of the turning engine drowned out what they were saying, but it was clear Cannon was arguing with the pilot. Overbee was unmoved. Cannon looked in our direction frantically and Pultman, in drag, did the same.

Anita and I moved as quickly as we could, but it wasn't quick enough. Pultman ran, and Overbee hesitated. People weren't supposed to run when you had a gun pointed at them. And he wasn't about to shoot a woman in the back.

"Bring him into the office," I shouted at Overbee.

He cupped his hand next to his ear and I shouted again. This time he got it and nodded his head.

"The car," I told Anita as Pultman, wig flying into the air, suitcase in hand, ran across the small airstrip.

We got to the Crosley and Anita sped after the killer with the suitcase. We passed Overbee who was guiding Cannon back to the wooden building. Overbee gave us a wave to let us know he had the man with the frightened look on his face under control.

"There he is," I said.

She turned a little to the right and caught him in our headlights. Pultman stopped, turned toward us, took my .38 out of his coat pocket, aimed, and pulled the trigger. He hit the right headlight. We closed in on him. He shot again. This time he missed partly because he was moving backwards, trying to decide whether to keep shooting or run for the line of trees about forty yards away.

He fired once more without really looking, and Anita pulled next to him. He was panting, makeup smeared on his face. He fired over his shoulder. Nothing. The gun was empty.

"Get ahead of him," I said.

She did, cutting him off. He stood panting, and I got out of the car. Anita turned the car so that the single headlight was on my back and in Pultman's eyes.

"You recognized my car back there," I said.

He nodded "yes," trying to catch his breath.

"Cannon an actor?"

He nodded "yes," and managed to get out, "I'll split it with you. Two ways, right down the middle. All in this suitcase. Count it out right here. You get the necklace. I get the ring."

"I'm independently wealthy," I said.

"Peters, don't be a fool."

"Can't help it," I said. "We're taking you in."

"Make sense," he said, stepping back. "Ask your girl-friend?"

He looked past me at Anita. Anita was out of the car and moving toward my side.

"How much?" she asked.

"About two hundred thousand for you two," Pultman said. "Well?"

"I just wanted to know how much we were turning down so I could tell my daughter," she said.

Pultman looked around for somewhere to run. He was worn out. I stepped toward him, trying to hide my limp. He was caught in the headlights, frozen.

I stood in front of him, and he put his hands up to cover his face from the punch he was sure was coming. I plucked my .38 from his hand, put it in my pocket, took the suitcase from him, and grabbed him by the neck.

"We've got some people to wake up," I said.

CHAPTER
13

ANITA AND I drove Pultman to the Wilshire station. He sat next to Anita in the front seat, his hands tied behind his back. I sat in the tiny space behind the seats, my arm draped around Pultman's neck. He didn't say anything, and I tried not to look at him. The makeup streaking his face made him look like a hungry zombie in a Monogram serial. Maybe we could get Pultman and Fiona together in the interrogation room at the Wilshire and they could have a little chat and touch up each other's makeup. But then again it was probably a better idea to keep them apart. I'd have to leave that decision to the police.

We ushered our prisoner to the desk sergeant—another old-timer, this one named Wilson—at a little before three in the morning. My ankle had settled into a steady throb.

"What's the cat drug in here, Peters?" he asked, peering over the top of his glasses.

"A badly accessorized murderer," I said. "You want to give Cawelti a call. Wake him up. Tell him I've got Pultman."

"Don't have to wake him unless he's asleep in the Squad Room," Wilson said. "He's doing a second shift from last night."

"Dedication," I said.

"You ask me, he doesn't like going home alone," Wilson said in a loud whisper. "I know the feeling."

"Thanks," I said.

Anita and I ushered Pultman up the wooden stairs and into the squad room. Even at three in the morning it wasn't empty, but it wasn't full, either. Thieves work nights, but your average domestic battle, strong-arm robbery, rape, and murder take place at civilized hours. Criminals need their sleep, too.

Two detectives were at their desks. One was on the phone. The other was John Cawelti looking as if he had just shaved and carefully combed his red hair right down the middle. He sat up and grinned.

"He's yours," I said.

"I demand my immediate release," said Pultman.

"You do?" asked Cawelti, getting up and moving to meet us.

"I've done nothing," Pultman said.

"Except dress up for Halloween on the wrong day and the wrong month," Cawelti said.

"I was on my way to a costume party," Pultman said.

"At two in the morning," Anita pointed out.

Cawelti looked at her, then at me, and smirked.

"This is Anita Maloney," I said. "Friend of mine."

I handed him the suitcase. He took it.

"That's my personal property," Pultman protested.

"Evidence," I said. "Papers, probably cash or bonds from Elsie Pultman's estate. Also," I said, taking the necklace and ring from my pocket and handing it to Cawelti, "the jewelry he took from Elsie Pultman's body a few hours ago."

"That was you," said Cawelti, looking at me. "I figured. You were the one at the cemetery."

"Me and Pultman," I said. "Bring in the caretaker."

"They've got his statement. We'll bring him in for a lineup." He turned to Pultman and smiled. If I were Pultman, I would not have liked that smile. "You dig up old ladies and steal their jewelry. A noble profession."

"First he kills them," I said. "You've got a Fiona Sullivan in custody. I think she can put a lid on this for you."

"I want a lawyer," Pultman said.

"First we go into a little room down the hall and have a chat," Cawelti said, taking his arm.

"I'll give you a statement," I said.

"Good. You do that, but right now I think Mr. Pultman is going with me to wash up, have a cup of coffee, and talk," said Cawelti. "I think Mr. Pultman . . . Jeffrey, is it? Jeffrey and I are going to come to an agreement and wrap this up."

"You were lucky, Peters," Pultman said.

"And you were too smart," I answered. "Too tricky. Too many loose ends. Too many games."

"I wanted it to be fun," said Pultman as Cawelti led him away. "And it was. Admit it. It was."

When they were through the squad room door Anita turned to me and said, "I think he's nuts."

"I think you're right," I said. "Maybe. Or maybe he's smart enough to already be thinking of claiming that he's nuts. Maybe he'll tell Cawelti that he hears voices that tell him to kill and dress up in women's clothes. Maybe that's what I would do if I were wearing a dress and my makeup was running."

"That kind of thing work?" Anita asked as we moved out of the squad room.

"Almost never," I said. "But he did enough nutty stuff to make a jury stop and think if it gets to a jury and if he gets a good criminal lawyer like Marty Leib."

Going down the stairs was harder on my ankle than going up had been. I grimaced. Anita put my arm around her shoulder.

"I guess this means our date is off for tonight," she said.

"What are you doing tomorrow night?"

"Going out for dinner and a movie?"

"Sounds good to me," I said.

She drove me to Mrs. Plaut's and helped me up the front stairs and through the door. We were four steps up the stairs to the second floor when Mrs. Plaut emerged from her rooms, blue robe wrapped around her with a purple sash, hands on her hips.

"Mr. Peelers," she said sternly.

How is it, I wondered not for the first time, that a woman as deaf as Irene Plaut could sense even a deep breath three rooms away through the walls but not hear someone knocking at her door?

"Mrs. Plaut," I said, turning to face her.

"You are drunk," she said, looking at Anita who was still holding my arm over her shoulder.

"No, Mrs. Plaut," I said. "I am hurt."

"What's wrong?"

"My ankle," I said. "Twisted."

She reached up and touched her ear. God was on my side. She was wearing her hearing aid, the one I had bought her, the one that spent most days and nights in a kitchen drawer next to her sterling silver.

"Twisted," she repeated with suspicion. "How?"

"I fell in a grave," I said.

"And who is this?" she went on, looking at Anita and apparently accepting without question the reason for my injury.

"Anita Maloney," I said. "A friend in need."

"She's not planning to stay the night," said Mrs. Plaut.

"There's almost no night left," I said.

"I'm not staying," Anita said. "I'll just take Mr. Peters to his room."

"Three minutes," said Mrs. Plaut.

"Less than two," answered Anita with a smile.

We started up the stairs again.

"You shouldn't be playing in graves at night," Mrs. Plaut said behind us. "You shouldn't be playing in graves at all. My great-uncle, Robert Stillwell, almost died in a grave in Remington, Kansas, during the War Between the States."

"Write it in your memoirs," I said.

"I will," answered Mrs. Plaut. "Breakfast is at 7:45."

We were at the top of the stairs now. I turned, my hands on the railing.

"I think I'll skip breakfast," I said.

"Southern pork fritters and eggs O'Bannion," she said. "I'll wake you."

"Thanks," I said.

Mrs. Plaut stood there, waiting.

"I can make it from here," I said to Anita. "Take my car. I'll pick it up in the morning at your place."

"Don't wake me," she said, leaning over to kiss my stubbly cheek.

"Mrs. Plaut is watching," I said.

"We'll have to live with the consequences," said Anita, starting down the stairs.

"You work for a living?" Mrs. Plaut asked as Anita neared the bottom of the stairs.

"Waitress," Anita said.

"Honest living," said Mrs. Plaut with approval. "I waited tables in Prescott, Arizona, for almost two years. Hard work. Rough talk. Bottom pinchers. Good tips. Long hours. Sore feet. I must inform you that sometimes Mr. Peelers is a scamp. At his age he should have chosen a steady job."

Anita looked up at me and said, "Maybe he'll pick one when he grows up."

"I doubt it," said Mrs. Plaut.

I went to my room, opened the door, flicked on the light, and managed to drag out my mattress and unroll it.

Dash sat watching me.

"Hungry?" I asked.

Dash, as usual, said nothing. I hobbled to the refrigerator, got some milk out, rinsed his bowl, filled it, and found a can of Spam. I opened the can, scooped some of it out, and put it on a plate for Dash who approached, smelled it, and started to eat. I put what was left in the refrigerator and staggered to the light switch.

That was all I remembered till Mrs. Plaut burst through the door at, according to the Beech-Nut clock on the wall, seven in the morning.

"Breakfast," she said.

I groaned.

"You have half an hour to shave, shower, put on clean clothing, and be at the table."

She closed the door and disappeared. I sat up. I was still

wearing Anita's ex-husband's clothes. Somehow I had taken my shoes off. My ankle was numb. My mouth felt like someone had scrubbed it with dry steel wool. I managed to get on my one good foot and one bad one and to kick off the clothes I was wearing. I found my ancient robe in the closet, put it on, and headed for the shared bathroom, hoping it wasn't occupied. It wasn't. Twenty minutes later, I was at Mrs. Plaut's table eating pork fritters, eggs O'Bannion, and drinking coffee.

Emma Simcox, Ben Bidwell, and Gunther all looked at me and waited. Mrs. Plaut had obviously said something about my early morning arrival with Anita.

"I fell in a grave," I explained.

"None of my business," said Bidwell, the one-armed car salesman. The customer was always right at Mad Jack's in Venice.

Miss Simcox smiled and bent her head.

"Toby, did you . . . ?" Gunther asked.

"We got him," I said. "I'll tell you all about it later. Doing anything for lunch?"

"I have an article to finish, Hungarian, very interesting. Something about using the sun as an energy source for automobiles instead of gasoline."

"Won't work," said Bidwell, the auto expert. "Mark my word. When the war is over, no one's gonna be interested in anything but cheap gas and fast cars."

"I shall mark your word," Gunther said politely. "I will be ready to lunch at one if that is not too late."

"Fine," I said.

"Pork fritters are great," said Bidwell.

Mrs. Plaut was not wearing her hearing aid this morning.

"Everything," she said solemnly, nibbling a slice of toast,

"is fate. We simply trust in the Lord, do our best, and join the war effort."

"Amen," said Emma Simcox.

"Amen," I added.

Westinghouse in the other room cackled something. It didn't sound like "amen."

After breakfast, I called for a cab and waited on the porch under Mrs. Plaut's framed autographed photograph of Eleanor Roosevelt. The sun was shining today. I should have gone to Doc Hodgdon for my ankle. I could do it later. First I had to pick up my car and get it to No-Neck Arnie.

Forty minutes later, I had managed to drive the one-eyed Crosley into Arnie's.

"What happened?" he asked.

"Someone shot the lamp out with my gun," I explained.

"I'll take a look," he said. "Give me ten minutes. You can wait around or give me a call."

"I'll call," I said.

I made my way slowly toward the open garage door.

"What happened to your leg?"

"Fell in a grave," I said.

"Got a pair of crutches in the office," he said. "When Nick fell in the grease pit the first time. I'll get 'em. No charge."

He came back with the crutches and handed them to me.

"Thanks, Arnie," I said.

"Stay out of open graves," he said and headed for my Crosley.

I waved a crutch at Manny as I passed Manny's Taco's. Manny waved back, showing no curiosity that I could see about my crutches. I continued on my pilgrimage to the Farraday Building. If my ankle had been up to it, I might have ducked Juanita, who was coming through the Farraday door humming something. I continued.

She didn't look any more surprised at my crutches than Manny.

"Was I right?" she asked.

I thought about her prophecy in the elevator when the whole thing had started. She had been right about everything but, as usual, it hadn't done me any good.

"Anything else to tell me?" I asked.

"You don't have to see a doctor. Your ankle's not broken. Just a sprain. Don't take the tape off for two days."

"As clear a prophecy as you've ever given me," I said.

"No prophecy," she answered, taking a compact out of her purse and examining herself in the mirror. "Remember the Vasquella brothers, the twins who come to see me on Tuesday mornings?"

"No."

"Well," she went on, touching her nose to smooth something out, "Manuel limped just like that. No swelling. Kept the tape on. He was fine in two days. How'd you hurt it?"

"Stepped on a dead woman in a grave," I said.

"Told you," she said with a wink before she jangled off.

The usual office noises and echoes greeted me in the Farraday lobby along with the familiar and comforting smell of Jeremy's Lysol. There was no possibility of my going up the stairs. I was happy to make it to the elevator, close the metal-grated doors, push the button, and lean back.

The sound of an off-key trombone slid by on the first floor. A duet of clacking typewriter and someone shouting in Spanish serenaded me on the second floor. By the time the elevator got to my floor, I had been treated to a symphony of less than pure delight.

When I opened the outer office, Violet looked up at me. So did a couple in the two waiting-room chairs. They were about seventy, looked scared, and were holding hands.

"What happened?" Violet asked.

"Tripped," I said, not wanting to go over it again.

"Rocky's coming home," she said eagerly.

"He's okay?"

"Perfect," Violet said. "His time's up. Says he doesn't think he wants to box anymore. Got the letter right here."

She held up a thin, blue, V-mail letter.

"Great," I said. "How soon?"

She shrugged.

"Soon is all I know."

"Soon is pretty good," I said.

"Pardon me," said the old woman. She had a European accent. "Are you Doctor Minck?"

"That's . . ." Violet began, but I cut her off.

"What seems to be the problem?"

"Mine husband. He has a tooth, a bad tooth. Maybe two bad teeth."

The man said something softly in whatever their language was and the woman nodded her head.

"What made you pick this office?" I asked.

"We were visiting cousin who is making zippers on this floor," she said. "We pass by, see the sign. I tell Max he must see tooth doctor now."

"I don't think I can work today," I said sadly, looking at my crutches. "There's a dentist two buildings down, across the street, name's Zanderoff. I think you'll be better off there."

The woman translated. The man said something.

"You sending us to different tooth doctor?"

"It's the right thing to do," I said. "I think you'd better get him over there right away."

The old man and woman got up, thanked me, and hurried out the door.

"You plan to tell Shelly?" I asked Violet.

She shook her head no.

Shelly came through the door and said, "Who were those two, the ones who just left here?"

"Foreigners. Wrong office," I said.

Shelly looked at Violet for confirmation. She said, "Foreigners. Wrong office."

Shelly walked past me through the door to his office. I followed him. He was wearing a green sports jacket, dark green slacks pulled high on his belly, and a fresh cigar. He adjusted his glasses and plucked an almost clean white dental apron from the rack near the door.

"We caught him, Shel," I said.

He turned to look at me, blinked, and said, "Sawyer?"

"His real name is Pultman," I said.

"You said 'we caught him'?"

"Anita Maloney and me," I said.

"Good. He shoot you in the ankle or kick you in the shin or something?"

"Something," I said.

"I think I deserve some credit here," Shelly said, moving his metal torture tool table and examining his weapons.

"You're definitely a hero, Shel," I said.

"A day's work," he said humbly.

"Fiona Sullivan was working with him," I said. "She isn't dead."

This got his attention. He turned in my direction and pointed a sharp metal object with a thin wire at the end.

"Hey," he said. "Hey. Then I'm not responsible for getting her killed."

"She's not dead," I said again.

"I've got a feeling this is gonna be one hell of a great day. Two fillings at nine. An extraction at ten. Braces on a kid at two. Full plate. Life is good, Toby. Life is good."

"It's great Shel," I said, heading for my office.

"I wanna show you something new I've been working on," he said, reaching toward something at the end of the metal table.

"Later," I said, not wanting to see what he was going to come up with. "I've got some calls to make."

Inside my office I opened my window, sat down behind my desk, and pulled out a pad of paper, a pen, and my bottle of Carter's Ink. My bill to Chaplin lacked only one thing, the price of fixing my headlight. I called Arnie. He told me what it would cost and I told him to fix it. Then I took out my notebook, looked at some of my expense notations, and composed my letter.

Dear Mr. Chaplin,

With the successful conclusion of the case for which you hired me, I herein submit my bill for services under our agreement of twenty-five dollars a day, plus twenty dollars a day for a protective agent.

Donation to the Eugene O'Neill Society of Southern California	$5
Two train compartments for San Francisco .	$49
Four days of investigation	$100
One day of protective service (Al Woodman)	$10

Gasoline $8
Cleaning of clothes (estimate soiled in
    cemetery) $3
Replacement of headlight (shot by
    criminal) $13.00
Miscellaneous (which I will itemize
    on request) $10.12
TOTAL. $200.12

Since you gave me a $200 advance, I owe you twelve
cents plus the cost of replacing the window in your house
and the lamp that Woodman shot. Let me know the cost
of the window. It's been a pleasure knowing you.

Sincerely,

Toby Peters

I took out my wallet and dug into my pockets. I put twelve
cents in an envelope, put Chaplin's name on it, and licked it
closed.

It was nine. I took a chance and called. A woman
answered.

"Mr. Chaplin, please," I said.

"He's just getting out of the shower, but who should I say
is calling?"

"Toby Peters."

"Toby," Chaplin said eagerly a few seconds later. "Any
news?"

"We got him," I said.

"Where?"

"Dressed in women's clothes and about to get on a char-
tered plane at two this morning."

"God, I wish I had been there."

"I don't think you'll have to give a statement," I said. "But I'm not sure.

"Can't be helped," he said with resignation. "This has been an amazing experience, one I'll not forget. This adventure has given me the inspiration to write a complete screenplay. It is no longer *Lady Killer*, but in honor of Mrs. Plaut I am calling it *Monsieur Verdoux*. I think calling it *Mister Voodoo* would be more apropos for an Abbott and Costello film, don't you think?"

"I do," I said. "I'd like to drop my bill off with you and ask you a favor."

"Name it," said Chaplin.

I told him.

"When?" he asked.

"This afternoon possible?"

"Can we make it tonight," he said. "I must take my wife to a luncheon at Janet Gaynor's. One can't afford to slight friends when one has so few."

"Tonight will be great. Name a time. I'll pick you up."

"No, I'll have a driver. I'll pick you up at Mrs. Plaut's at, shall we say, six?"

"Six is fine."

"Oh, by the way," he said. "How much do I owe you? I'll have it with me in cash."

"You gave me a two-hundred-dollar advance. I owe you twelve cents," I said. "Plus the cost of your window and lamp."

"Let's call it even," he said.

"Let's," I agreed.

"See you at six."

I hung up, tore open the envelope, pocketed the dime and

two pennies, and sat back. Twenty minutes or so later, while I was picking through old mail and paying a few small bills, Jeremy came in.

"Sheldon tells me you caught Pultman," he said.

"For once, Sheldon is right. Thanks for your help, Jeremy."

"You are welcome. I've finished a poem about Juanita. Extraordinary woman. Would you like to hear it?"

"Absolutely," I said.

He stood and read:

No-nonsense sanctum, four unmatched chairs and a
table,
Behind a door that says "Juanita," next to Albert Dew
A baby photographer who has no patience with chil-
dren who
Find him unfunny and smelly too. His clients are few.
On the other side of Juanita are two brothers named
Whales
Whose income is derived from whoopee cushion sales.
Maintaining class in company such as this
Is but a consummation devoutly to be wished.
But Juanita, born Jewish in the Bronx, has a long list
Of Mexicans, Negroes, Creoles, and others who exist
To hear her in Brooklynese unrepentant and pure
Tell their future in words and images obscure.
Juanita's power came unbidden, gift and curse,
For her thoughts, images, fragments come in a burst
Never quite clear in their meaning
Till in hours or days the future becomes the beginning.
"Do not eat meat today and stay away from green,"
She told me yesterday riding the rickety Farraday ele-
vator.

"I don't eat meat," I said, "and I'll avoid the green."
"You can't," she sighed. "Only when passed is it seen."
"Then what good does it do to know?"
Her long earrings dangled as she turned quite slow.
"I don't understand," she said. "I only see.
Do you know who Cassandra was?" She looked at me.
"A poor Greek shiksa who couldn't keep her mouth shut.
No one believed her. They thought she was a nut.
It's the seer," she said, patting my cheek.
"We know what we're saying, but to you it's all Greek."
The elevator creaked doors open at the fourth floor.
"My curse, my blessing. As the raven once said, Evermore."

"I like it," I said.

Jeremy handed me the neatly printed copy of the poem. I put it on the desk.

"But that encounter yesterday was not the end. At lunch I almost choked on a Brussels sprout. You see the irony in her vision? I eat no meat and came close to death from a green vegetable."

"What happened?"

"I punched myself in the stomach. The Brussels sprout came out."

"There's a moral in this somewhere," I said.

"There's a meaning too deep to penetrate," he said seriously.

"That's life," I said.

"Precisely," said Jeremy. "Precisely."

EPILOGUE

CHAPLIN CAME EXACTLY at six in a black limo with tinted windows. He got out of the car and smiled at me. He was wearing a gray suit and vest and a perfectly matched tie. His shoes were polished and bright.

"Is dear Mrs. Plaut in?" he asked.

"She's in," I said.

"Excellent."

I followed him inside where he knocked at Mrs. Plaut's door. Westinghouse went mad inside. And then the door opened.

"Mr. Voodoo," she said, holding out her hands.

Chaplin took both of them and said, "My dear, I have engaged in a charade. I'm not Mr. Voodoo. I am Charlie Chaplin. Truly."

Mrs. Plaut looked at him for a moment and then said,

"How wonderful. I'll have to tell my friends. I love your movies."

"Thank you for your inspiration and hospitality. I savored your sweetbread and tongue delight."

"You are very welcome," she said, removing her hands from his.

"We must be going now," he said. "If you would accept an autographed photograph, it would be my pleasure to send you one."

"I'd love it," she said. "I'll put it in a frame on the porch right next to Eleanor Roosevelt."

Chaplin bowed and walked out the door in front of me. I started to hobble after him on my crutches, but Mrs. Plaut whispered, "Mr. Peelers."

I turned to her.

"Mr. Voodoo is a crazy man. I think he's harmless but you never can tell. The man looks nothing like Charlie Chaplin. Be cautious."

"I'll be cautious," I said.

I went out the door and caught up with Chaplin at the car. When I got into the back seat with him, I gave the uniformed driver the address.

There was a black hat box next to Chaplin.

"What's that?" I asked.

"That?" he said, looking at the box as if he had never seen it before. "That, I don't know what that is."

We drove to North Hollywood and the driver parked directly in front of my brother's small house. Chaplin and I got out and went to the door.

"Oh, I forgot something," Chaplin said hurrying back to the car.

My nephew, Dave, opened the door. His brother, Nate, and two-year-old sister, Lucy, were right behind him.

"Uncle Toby," shouted Nate. "Mom, Dad, Uncle Toby's here."

I stood in the doorway waiting for Chaplin.

Phil and Ruth came from the direction of the dining room. Ruth moved slowly. There didn't seem to be much left of her.

"Don't stand there," Phil said. "Come in and close the door."

"I brought someone to see you, Ruth," I said.

"Brought someone?"

She looked at Phil, who shook his head to show that he had no idea of what or who I was talking about. Chaplin was taking a long time for whatever he had forgotten.

"He's getting something out of the car. He'll be right here," I said.

"Is it a killer?" Nate asked hopefully.

"No," I said. "It's . . ."

I heard a movement behind me. Ruth's mouth fell open.

"Oh my God," she said.

I turned and saw the Little Fellow. Derby, mustache, tight jacket, baggy pants, cane, and oversized shoes. He took off his hat and smiled at Ruth. From behind his back he pulled a single flower, a violet. He stepped past me and handed it to her.

Lucy began to cry. Phil picked her up.

"Ah, one more thing if I may," Chaplin said, reaching inside his jacket.

He pulled out a framed photograph of himself as the Tramp and gave it to Ruth who read the inscription:

233

*To Ruth Pevsner, with love, respect and hope.
Affectionately, Charlie Chaplin.*

Ruth clutched the flower and photograph to her chest.

Chaplin doffed his hat again and went out the door. We walked after him and watched him waddle away, twirling his cane, and get into the limo.

The baby had stopped crying and was watching, as were her brothers.

"Toby," Ruth said. "Toby."

She gave me a hug.

"I've got to go," I said. "I've got a date with Anita."

"Call her up," said Phil. "Tell her to take a cab here if she wants. I'll pay for it. We're having a late dinner."

"Okay," I said. "Thanks."

"Least I can do for my brother," he said.